Vipers' Tangle

Books in the Loyola Classics Series

Amy Welborn, general editor

The Devil's Advocate
by Morris L. West

Do Black Patent Leather Shoes Really Reflect Up?
by John R. Powers

The Edge of Sadness
by Edwin O'Connor

Helena
by Evelyn Waugh

In This House of Brede
by Rumer Godden

The Last Catholic in America
by John R. Powers

Mr. Blue
by Myles Connolly

Saint Francis
by Nikos Kazantzakis

Vipers' Tangle
by François Mauriac

Vipers' Tangle

FRANÇOIS MAURIAC

Introduction by Robert Coles

LOYOLA CLASSICS
CHICAGO

LOYOLAPRESS.
3441 N. ASHLAND AVENUE
CHICAGO, ILLINOIS 60657
(800) 621-1008
WWW.LOYOLAPRESS.ORG

Originally published in French under the title *Le Noeud de Vipères,* 1932. This translation by Gerard Hopkins was first published in 1951.

Cover illustration by Jerry Bingham

Series art direction: Adam Moroschan
Series design: Adam Moroschan and Erin VanWerden
Cover design: Erin VanWerden
Interior design: Erin VanWerden

Library of Congress Cataloging-in-Publication Data
Mauriac, François, 1885–1970.
  [Nœud de vipères. English]
  Vipers' tangle / by François Mauriac ; translated by Gerard Hopkins.
     p. cm. — (Loyola classics series)
  This translation originally published: 1951.
  ISBN 0-8294-2211-0
  I. Hopkins, Gerard, 1892– II. Title. III. Series.
PQ2625.A93N613 2005
843'.912—dc22

                                          2005006951

Printed in the United States of America
05 06 07 08 09 10 Bang 10 9 8 7 6 5 4 3 2 1

Introduction

Robert Coles

In 1964, several hundred American college students, along with some of their teachers (graduate students and even a handful of tenured professors), assembled in Mississippi for a summer of political activity. The intention was to work at "voter registration"—a term that meant more than enabling individuals to fill out forms. It was, at a deeper level, an all-out effort to take on the bastion of segregation, beginning with the polite but firm request that thousands of Americans be allowed to cast ballots along with their fellow citizens.

At that time, African Americans were not allowed to vote in the Magnolia state and elsewhere across the South. Now relatively privileged white youths were intent on changing that legal, social, and racial state of affairs, and in so doing, alter significantly a nation's politics. During that summer, the students read books they had brought with them, mostly social-science texts that tried to tell it like it then was throughout Dixie. The books were handed along from person to person, and later there were discussions—questions, answers, surmises, and refutations.

One afternoon as we all sat sweating and considering the world we'd come to witness (and very much wished to change), we made mention of the psychological and sociological analyses we'd been finding in the books we'd been attending, contemplating hard and long together. Our line of inquiry, of shared reflection, was abruptly stopped in its tracks by words I've never forgotten, spoken by a college student who had been majoring in French literature and hoped to do a thesis on a French novelist then very much alive (indeed, twelve years earlier, in 1952, he'd won the Nobel Prize). "I wish we would read *Vipers' Tangle*," he urged. He then gave a spirited presentation of what François Mauriac had offered in that novel published in 1932—"a tough dissection of privilege and power, of ambition and greed and hypocrisy," our student-become-teacher declared. We all sat there enthralled, a bit taken aback—indeed, even today, more than forty years later, when I hear that moment, courtesy of my tape recorder, I feel roused to thought.

A novel's relentless evocation of a distant nation's bourgeoisie became a challenge to us, a summons to look carefully at what and who we were and why we were there. (We who had so much going for ourselves, even as we worried so earnestly about the disenfranchised around us and, not to mention, the working-class white folks in Mississippi, who in substantial number were not loath to point out our relative privilege and, too, the smug sense of exemplary virtue we were in danger of demonstrating. I remember one man in particular who said, "You folks come down here pointing fingers at us—I only hope when you get back, you'll take a good, close look around and see what you've got going for yourself and what's no good for others. See who has to work like hell and pick up the tab for you people, through their sweat, just like you keep saying our colored people here do for us.")

Soon thereafter, a few of us began reading *Vipers' Tangle* and, with each page, realizing some of the social and economic truths that Mississippian, for his own reasons, had been pressing upon us. One student, upon finishing the novel, mentioned Sinclair Lewis, his insistent, sometimes scorching examination of our Main Streets and Babbitts. Still, Mauriac, we all agreed, could be more affecting (and disturbing) because he was not interested in brisk satire; rather, he let his novel explore a character's vigorously pursued and often lonely life. In fact, before the story of *Vipers' Tangle* begins, the author asks his reader to "feel pity and be moved by his [the character's] predicament"—no doubt a warning of sorts: the idea being that doubt and considerate exploration can prompt kindness, in contrast with the jabs here, the shaking of the head there, that full-fledged satire offers.

To be sure, Louis—sixty-eight years old, sick and dying, writing of his life, calling forth its ups and downs—is not without scorn for others, even for the Catholic Church, for his wife of forty years, and for the family to which she belonged. The point of the novel is to look at the way an individual's will interacts with chance and circumstance. What have been the consequences of his choices? What kind of life has resulted? What has been missed?

This man who has withheld so much from his family now speaks and speaks, in the form of a bitter letter to his wife, of the greed and self-importance of others, through which is revealed his own sin, his own yearning for money and power and the privileges and perquisites that a rise in class can bring. Yes, the more this dying man renders the "unreflecting ego-ism," to use George Eliot's words, in others, the nearer we get (with no authorial shove or exploratory asides) to the story's narrator, no mean self-critic, even as he levels away at the pre-tenses and hypocrisy of those he, nevertheless, aimed so long and hard to join through the binding bonds of family life.

We learn of that life, the conceits and deceits of the French middle to upper bourgeoisie, its landed-gentry version, near Bordeaux, where Mauriac was born in 1885. We learn, alas, of the costs exacted by a developed, ever-present, and ready canni-ness. So it happens with our friends, our family members, who become objects of avarice, of calculation, of use and abuse, of yearning for that ultimate secular sanction, the dough that comes from an inheritance—which is the book's big subject:

who will get what, and when, from this dying man who is frank to tell us of his wrongdoing of mind and heart, and yes, soul. "I could touch my guilt," he confides, and then this confessional self-arraignment: "It was not only that my heart had become a nest of vipers, that it had been filled with hatred for my children, with a lust for vengeance and a grasping love of money. What was worse than that was that I had refused to look beyond the tangle of vile snakes. I had treasured their knotted hideousness as though it had been the central reality of my being—as though the beating of the life blood in my veins had been the pulse of all those swarming reptiles."

Lest we dwell only on our aging character's self-incrimination, we are reminded in no uncertain terms that he had busily pursued a given world—it can be said that his creator, François Mauriac, intends for us to take that world's moral pulse through his character's remarks: "Once, in the dark hours, in a moment of self-deprecation, I had compared my heart to a knot of vipers. How wrong I had been! The knot of vipers was outside myself."

Here is a novelist who knows his Bible well; who wrote in 1936, four years after *Vipers' Tangle* was published, *Vie de Jésus;* who gives us St. Teresa of Ávila as his companion psychologist before his own words begin; who wrote at length about Pascal, whose 277th Pensée declares that "the heart has its reasons, which reason does not know," and who followed in the 278th

Pensée with "it is the heart which experiences God, not reason." Even as Pascal turned to St. Augustine, his confessional mode of searching for spiritual truth, so does Mauriac in *Vipers' Tangle* connect us to the unembarrassed craving of those two spiritual predecessors—who dared wish that through their own psychological twists and turns there would somehow come the spiritual peace it is our human destiny to keep trying to find for ourselves, but which happens only by God's grace.

This moment of grace is veiled and never directly described by Mauriac. But we can see how the space has been opened in Louis's heart: through confrontation with death, in a meeting with a son who seems to embody the worst of his own character, perhaps even through the sacrifices of his little daughter who, years before, as she lay struck by typhoid fever, managed to murmur her wish to die "for Papa."

Mauriac's brilliant exploration of Louis's soul might discourage us with its vivid portrait of the destructive obsessions that can blind us to love and waste so much of the precious time we have on earth. As we read *Vipers' Tangle,* it is impossible to avoid looking in the mirror, perhaps in regret. However, the power of the novel lies in the moments that we, like Louis, can put the mirror down and open ourselves to the hope and grace always at hand and in the realization that it is never too late for redemption.

A man about to die finds life, responding at last to that which has urged him on, haunted him, eluded him, and finally, come to him as a great presence, holding him, a self-described "monster," in its everlasting arms. A dying man who has been like a Notre Dame gargoyle, surveying the city below, now finds the way to come to life by opening himself to the Unseeable and immersing himself, as God did through Jesus, in the pain and joy of his fellow human beings. All that the word *viper* suggests—to be shrewd, devious, sneaky, deceptive, tricky, a double dealer—now comes to a kind of naught through the workings of redemptive confession: a heart seized by a knot of vipers is now free, free at last, so that the one in whom it beat all those long years can reach out heartfully toward his fellow human beings, as he himself has been embraced.

Robert Coles is a professor of psychiatry and medical humanities at the Harvard Medical School and the James Agee Professor of Social Ethics at Harvard University. His books include the Pulitzer Prize–winning Children of Crisis *series as well as* The Spiritual Life of Children *and* The Call of Stories.

Vipers' Tangle

PART ONE

"... Consider, O God, that we are without understanding of ourselves; that we do not know what we would have and set ourselves at an infinite distance from our desires. ..."

St. Teresa of Ávila

The man here depicted was the enemy of his own flesh and blood. His heart was eaten up by hatred and by avarice. Yet, I would have you, in spite of his baseness, feel pity and be moved by his predicament. All through his dreary life, squalid passions stood between him and that radiance that was so close that an occasional ray could still break through to touch and burn him: not only his own passions, but, primarily, those of the lukewarm Christians who spied upon his actions, and whom he himself tormented. Too many of us are similarly at fault, driving the sinner to despair and blinding his eyes to the light of truth.

It was not money that this miser really treasured, nor, in his blind fury, was it vengeance that he sought. What it was that he truly loved you may discover who have the strength of mind, and the courage, to follow his story to the end, to that ultimate moment of confession that death cut short.

I

When you find this letter lying on top of a bundle of securities in my safe you will be surprised. I might have been better advised to entrust it to my solicitor, with instructions to hand it to you after my death, or to leave it in that locked drawer of my desk that my children will almost certainly force before my body has grown cold. But for years I have written and rewritten it in my imagination and always, in my bouts of sleeplessness, have seen it staring at me from the shelf of a safe empty of everything except this single act of vengeance upon which I have been brooding for almost half a century.

You need not be afraid. As a matter of fact, any cause for fear that you might have had will have been dissipated before you read these lines. "The securities are there all right!" I can hear your raised voice in the hall as you announce the good news on your return from the bank. "The securities are there all right!" you'll say to the children through the folds of your mourning veil.

But you've had a very narrow escape! I had taken all the necessary steps. Had I so willed it, you would stand today stripped of everything but the house and lands. You can thank your lucky stars that I have outlived my hatred. For years I believed that it was the most vital part of me. But now, quite suddenly, and for the time being, at least, it has ceased to mean anything to me. I find it difficult in my old age to recapture the vindictive mood of earlier years when I would lie in my sickbed, night after night, not so much planning the method of revenge (the delay-action bomb had already been "set" with an attention to detail that was a matter of considerable pride to me) as wondering how I might derive the maximum of satisfaction from its detonation. I wanted to live just long enough to see your faces when you got back from the bank. It was merely a matter of not giving you authority to open the safe too soon, of waiting just long enough to enjoy the sound of your despairing question—"but where *are* the securities?" I felt that no death pangs, however frightful, could spoil that pleasure for me. Of such calculating malice was I capable! And yet, by nature I am not a monster. How came it, then, that I was brought to such a pass?

It is four o'clock, and my luncheon tray is still standing on the table, with flies buzzing round the dirty plates. I have rung, but with no result. Bells never work in the country. I am lying quite patiently in this room where I slept as a child, and where, no doubt, I shall die. When that moment comes, the first thought of our dear daughter Geneviève will be to claim it for her children. It is the largest in the house and has the best outlook. It has been earmarked entirely for my own use. You will, I hope, do me the justice to admit that I did offer to move out in Geneviève's favor and would have done so had not Dr. Lacaze expressed the opinion that the dampness of the ground floor might be bad for my bronchitis. I have no doubt that I should have been as good as my word: but I should have harbored such a sense of grievance that the doctor's refusal to countenance the change was, perhaps, fortunate. All through my life I have made sacrifices, and the memory of them has poisoned my mind, nourishing and fattening the kind of rancorous resentment that grows worse with the passage of the years.

The love of quarreling is, with us, a family trait. I have often heard my mother say that my father quarreled with his parents, and that they themselves died without ever again setting eyes on the daughter whom they had driven from home thirty years earlier (she married and produced that brood of Marseilles cousins with whom we have never had anything to do). None of us ever knew the rights and wrongs of the squabble, but we took the hatreds of our forebears so wholeheartedly on trust that if I ran across one of those Marseilles cousins in the street today, I should turn my back on him. But, after all, one needn't have anything to do with one's distant relations. It is a very different matter with wives and children. No doubt united families *do* exist: but when I think of the number of households in which two individuals live a life of constant exasperation and mutual loathing, forever sitting at the same table, using the same washbasin, lying between the same sheets, it is really remarkable how few divorces there are! They live in a constant state of mutual detestation, yet can never escape an enforced proximity!

Why should I have felt the itch to scribble on my birthday? I am entering on my sixty-eighth year, but no one else knows it. There are always cakes and flowers and little candles for Geneviève and Hubert and their children when birthdays come round. . . . If I have never, for years past, given you anything on yours, that is not because I have overlooked it. No, it is my form of revenge, and I get a certain satisfaction from it. . . . The last bunch of birthday flowers that ever came my way was picked by the crippled fingers of my poor mother. In order to get them, she had, in spite of her weak heart, paid one last, painful visit to the rose garden.

Where was I? Oh, yes, you will doubtless be wondering why I have been suddenly seized by this mania for writing. "Mania" is the right word. You can judge of its strength from the way all the letters lean the same way, like pine trees under the impact of a westerly wind. Listen: I began this letter by referring to a vengeance on which I had long brooded but now renounce. There is, however, something in you, some part *of* you, that I long to overcome—your silence. Don't mistake my meaning. You have a ready enough tongue and can talk about poultry and vegetables for hours on end with Cazau. With the children, even with the youngest of them, you can jabber, day after day, until I can scarcely hear myself think. Many's the time I have got up from the table with my head feeling as empty as a rotten nut, obsessed by business cares and worries of every kind, which I could not share with a soul . . . especially after the Villenave case, which led to my being recognized (to quote the newspapers) as a "great Criminal Pleader." The more tempted I was to believe in my own importance, the more determined did you seem to make me feel my insignificance. . . . But it's not that I am referring to now. The silence I want to get my own back on is of quite a different kind. It comes of your determined refusal ever to discuss our own affairs, our own utter failure to understand one another. Many and many a time, watching a play or reading a novel, I find myself wondering whether, in actual fact, there ever *are* lovers or married couples who have "scenes," who lay all their cards on the table and find relief in unburdening their hearts.

For forty years we have suffered side by side. In the whole of that time you have always managed to avoid saying anything that went below the surface, have always avoided committing yourself.

I believed at one time that this attitude of yours was deliberate, the expression of some fixed determination the reason for which escaped me. And then, quite suddenly, I realized the truth—which was that discussions of the kind I longed for just didn't interest you. So utterly alien was I from all your concerns, that you shied away, not because you were frightened but because you were bored. You became an expert at scenting danger and could see me coming a mile off. If, sometimes, I managed to take you by surprise, either you succeeded, without difficulty, in avoiding the issue, or you patted my cheek, gave me a kiss, and made for the door.

I might have some reason to fear that, having read thus far, you will tear this letter up and read no farther. But somehow I don't think that is likely to happen. For some time now I have caught you looking at me with a certain amount of surprise and curiosity. You may not be very observant where I am concerned, but even you can hardly fail to have noticed a change in my mood. I feel pretty well assured that, this time, you will not avoid the issue. I want you to know, you and the rest of your brood, your son, your daughter, your son-in-law, and your grandchildren, what manner of man it is who has lived out his solitary existence in your midst and against whom you have closed your ranks; the overworked lawyer who has had to be handled with tact because he held the purse strings but whose sufferings might have been those of somebody living on a different planet. What planet? It has never occurred to you to try to find out. Don't be alarmed. I am no more concerned here to compose an advance obituary of myself than to draw up a brief for the prosecution in the case of me versus you. The one outstanding quality of my mind—which would have impressed itself on any other woman—is a terrifying lucidity.

I have never possessed the power of self-deception that is most men's standby in the struggle for existence. When I have acted basely, I have always known precisely what I was doing. . . .

At this point I had to break off . . . no one brought me a lamp or came to close the shutters. . . . I sat here looking out at the roof of the bottling shed, the tiles of which are as vivid in color as flowers or the breasts of birds. I could hear the thrushes in the ivy on the Carolina poplar and the noise made by somebody rolling a cask. I am fortunate in being able to wait for death in the one spot of all the world where everything is as I remember it, the sole difference being that the stutter of a motor engine has replaced the creaking of the old bucket-and-chain well worked by a donkey. (And of course, there's the loathsome mail plane that announces teatime and leaves its horrible smear across the sky.)

Few men are lucky enough to be able to find again in their actual physical surroundings, and within their range of vision, the world that most discover only if they have the courage and the patience to search their memories. . . . I lay my hand on my chest and feel the beating of my heart. I look at the glass-fronted medicine cupboard containing the hypodermic syringe, the little bottle of nitrite of amyl, and such other odds and ends as might be needed should I have one of my attacks. Would anybody hear me if I called? You're all so insistent that it's only a *false angina,* not so much because you want to convince *me,* but because you'd like to believe it yourselves and so feel justified in sleeping soundly at night. I am breathing more easily now. It is exactly as though a hand were gripping my left shoulder and keeping it rigid in a strained position so that I may never be allowed to forget, for a moment, what's lying in wait for me. In my case, death certainly won't come by stealth. It has been snuffing round me for years. I can hear it and feel its breath. It treats me with patience because I make no effort to resist, because I submit to the discipline that its approach imposes. I am ending my life in a dressing gown, surrounded by all the paraphernalia of incurable disease, sunk in the great winged chair where my mother sat waiting for her end. There is a table beside me, as there was beside her, laden with medicine bottles. I am ill shaven and evil smelling, a slave to all sorts of disgusting little habits. But don't be too sure. In the intervals between attacks I am my old self. Bourru, the solicitor, who thought me as good as gone, has got used to seeing me turn up as hale and hearty as ever, and I can still spend hours in the safe-deposit vault, snipping off dividend coupons unaided.

I must manage to live long enough to complete this confession, to *make* you listen. During all the years in which I shared your bed, you never failed, each time I got in beside you, to say—"I'm simply *dropping*, I'm half-asleep already. . . ."

It was less my endearments than my words that you were trying to avoid.

True, our unhappiness began with the sort of interminable discussions that are the delight of young married couples. We were little more than children. I was twenty-three, you eighteen, and perhaps love was less of a pleasure to us than the confidences, the talks, in which we gave free play to all our thoughts. Like young children in their earliest friendships, we had sworn to tell one another everything. So little had I to confess that I was driven to elaborate and embellish such squalid little adventures as had come my way, nor did it ever occur to me that your experience had been any fuller than my own. I never dreamed that, before I came into your life, you might have murmured another man's name to yourself, and in this belief I continued, until . . .

It was in this very room where I sit writing now. The wallpaper has been changed, but the mahogany furniture still stands precisely where it did then. There was then, as now, a tumbler of iridescent glass upon the table, along with a tea set that had been won in a raffle. Moonlight flooded the matting, and the south wind, blowing across the Landes, brought the smell of heath fires to our very bedside.

That night you spoke once more of Rodolphe—the old friend whom you had often mentioned, and always in the dusk of our room, as though you wanted to make sure that his ghost should be between us in the moments of our closest union. Have you forgotten? It was not enough for you now merely to mention his name.

"There are things, darling, I ought to have told you before we got engaged. I feel rather guilty about having kept them back—not that there was ever anything the least bit serious—so please don't start worrying. . . ."

I was quite easy in my mind and did nothing to provoke a confession. But you forced it on me. So eager were you to tell me the whole story that, at first, I felt rather embarrassed. It wasn't that you wanted to ease your conscience: it wasn't that you felt you owed it me to make a clean breast of this particular chapter in your past—though that was the reason you gave, and that was what I think you really believed.

No, the truth of the matter was that you were reveling in a delicious memory. You could no longer resist the sweet temptation. Perhaps you suspected that the incident might constitute a possible threat to our happiness. However that may be, the whole thing was, as they say, beyond your power to control. The shadow of this Rodolphe hung over our marriage bed, and there was nothing you could do about it.

But I don't want you to run away with the idea that our unhappiness started in jealousy. Later, it is true, I was to become furiously jealous, but I certainly felt nothing remotely resembling that passion on the summer night of '85 that I am now recalling, the night on which you confessed that, while on holiday at Aix, you had become engaged to this unknown young man.

How odd to think that I should have had to wait forty-five years before explaining what I felt about it all! I am not even sure that you will read this letter. The whole thing is of so little interest to you. *My* concerns are, to you, sheer boredom. Very early on, the children began to come between us, so that you neither saw nor heard me, and now there are the grand-children. . . . Well, it can't be helped. I am going to make this one last effort. It may be that I shall exert greater power over you when I am dead than I ever did while living . . . anyhow, at first. For a few weeks I shall once again occupy a place in your life. If only as a matter of duty you will read these pages to the end. That I *must* believe. I do.

II

As I have said, at the time of your confession I felt no jealousy. How am I to make you understand what it was that it destroyed in me?

I was the only child of the woman whom you knew as a widow, or, rather, in whose society you lived for many long years without ever really knowing her at all. But even if you had been sufficiently interested to try to discover the precise nature of the bond uniting that particular mother and that particular son, I doubt whether you would have succeeded in doing so. *You* were one of the many component cells of a powerful and numerous middle-class family, one element in a hierarchy, one cog in a highly organized machine. You could not begin to grasp the extent to which the widow of a minor official at the prefecture could be wrapped up in a son when he was all that she had left to her. She took pride in my school successes, and in them I, too, found all my happiness. At that time I was fully convinced that we were very poor. The evidence was all around me, in the narrow pattern of our lives, in the strict economy that my mother made the law of our being. Not that I was allowed to want for anything. I realize today how spoiled I was as a child. My mother's farms, at Hosteins, furnished us with a quantity of inexpensive food, and I should have been much surprised had I been told that it was of exceptional quality. Corn-fed chickens, hares, goose pâté, were not my idea of luxury. I had always heard it said that our land was of no great value, and, indeed, when my mother came into her inheritance it had consisted only of stretches of grassland on which my grandfather, as a child, had herded cattle. What I did not know was that my parents' first care had been to make it productive, and that at twenty-one I should find myself the owner of two thousand hectares of mature timber already yielding a great number of pit-props. My mother managed, also, to save some part of her modest income. Even during my father's lifetime, the two of them had "bled themselves white" so as to be able to buy Calèse (forty thousand francs they paid for those vineyards, which now I wouldn't part with for a million!). We lived in the Rue Sainte-Catherine, on the third floor of a house belonging to us (it had, together with a number of vacant lots, formed my father's inheritance). Twice each week we received a hamper from the country. My mother went as seldom as possible to the butcher. The only ambition I had at that time was to enter the École Normale. There was a battle royal on Thursdays and Sundays before I could be induced to take a little exercise in the fresh air. I was not in the least like those boys who are always head of the class without any apparent effort. I was a "swot" and proud of it: just a common or garden plodder. I cannot remember ever having taken the least pleasure, while at school, in studying Virgil or Racine. They were "set books" for me and nothing more. I segregated from among the achievements of the human spirit such subjects as formed part of the curriculum—no others seemed to me to have the slightest importance—and wrote just the sort of essays that one had to write in order to satisfy the examiners: in other words, precisely what had already been written by generations of candidates. That was the kind of little idiot I was, and probably would have continued to be, but for an attack of blood spitting, which terrified my mother and, two months before the École Normale entrance examination, compelled me to abandon all hope of my chosen career.

That was the price I had to pay for an overworked childhood and an unhealthy adolescence. A growing youth cannot, with impunity, sit crouched over a table far into the night and despise all forms of physical exercise. Am I boring you? I am terrified of boring you. You mustn't skip a line. You must take my word for it that I am confining myself strictly to the essentials of my story. The drama of our two lives, yours and mine, was conditioned by things that happened to me as a young man, things you never knew or, having known, promptly forgot.

At any rate, these first few pages will have shown you that I have no intention of letting myself off easily—and that must be not a little satisfying to your hatred. . . . Please don't protest. . . . If you have begun to think about me now, it is solely in the hope of finding nourishment for your hostility.

I don't want to be unjust in my attitude to the undersized and sickly creature whom I left, just now, poring over his lexicons. When I read other men's recollections of childhood, and take notice of the paradise that seems to fascinate their backward gaze, I cannot help feeling a sharp spasm of pain. "How about myself?" I ask; "why this sense of a wasteland ever since my earliest years? Maybe I have forgotten what these others remember: maybe I, too, trailed clouds of glory. . . ." But, alas, I can recall nothing but desperate struggles, nothing but the embittered rivalry in which I was involved with one chap called Hennoch and another called Rodrigue. I instinctively repulsed all friendly advances. There were some, I remember, on whom the prestige of my successes exerted a species of attraction, so that they were fascinated by my very churlishness. I did not suffer affection gladly: I had a horror of "sentiment."

Were I a professional writer, I could not compose a single "touching" passage from the record of my school years. . . . But wait, I *do* recollect one incident, trivial though it may appear. I recalled very little about my father, but there were moments at which I felt convinced that he was not really dead at all, but only that, as the result of a combination of circumstances, he had somehow vanished. On such occasions I would run all the way along the Rue Sainte-Catherine on my way home from school, keeping to the middle of the road, and dodging the traffic, because I was afraid that the crowded pavement would slow me down. I would take the stairs four at a time—only to find my mother darning by the window and the photograph of my father hanging in its usual place to the right of my bed. Then, scarcely responding to my mother's kiss, I would settle down to my books.

After the blood-spitting incident, which changed the whole pattern of my future, I spent several melancholy months in a cottage at Arcachon. The ruin of my health had put a full stop to any hope of a university career. My poor mother got on my nerves. She seemed to take no account of my changed circumstances and to be wholly unconcerned about what was to happen to me. Each day, she lived for "thermometer time." All her sorrow, all her joy, seemed to hang upon the record of my weekly weighings. When, later, it was my fate to lead the life of an invalid, without anybody showing the least interest in the state of my health, I realized that I was suffering the just punishment for my hardness of heart, for the unyielding resentment of the spoiled child that I had shown in those earlier years.

With the first of the fine weather I began, as my mother put it, to "look up." Indeed, I was like somebody reborn. I broadened out and grew stronger. My body had suffered cruelly from the discipline I had imposed upon it, but now, in the dry air of the forest, with its furze and arbutus, which surrounded Arcachon in the days when it was no more than a village, it began to put forth new blossoms of health.

About this time, I learned from my mother that there was no need for me to worry about the future; that we were the possessors of a handsome fortune that was increasing year by year. I could well afford to wait, since, almost certainly, I should be released from military service. All my masters had been struck by my unusual fluency in speaking. My mother was anxious for me to read law and seemed convinced that, without fatiguing myself unduly, I could easily become a success at the bar, unless, of course, I felt attracted to politics. . . . On and on she talked, pouring out all her plans for me, and I sat there listening, in a mood of sulky hostility, staring out of the window.

I began to run after women. Noticing this new development, my mother adopted an attitude of frightened tolerance. In later years, as a result of living in close contact with your relations, I have learned how seriously sexual irregularities are regarded in religious families. The only thing that worried my mother was the possible ill effect of such indulgences on my health. Once she was assured that I was being reasonably careful she shut her eyes to my nocturnal outings, though always stipulating that I should be home by midnight. Don't be afraid that I am going into the details of my amorous adventures. I know how all that side of life disgusts you, and, anyhow, they were too trivial and too squalid to deserve recording.

But this I will say, that even in those early days I paid a high price for them. I suffered from the fact that I was deficient in charm, that my youthfulness paid such poor dividends. It was not, I think, that I was ill looking. My features were "regular," and Geneviève, who is the living image of me, was very pretty as a girl. No, my trouble was that I am one of those who, in popular parlance, have never known what it is to be young. There had been an overplus of gloom, a lack of freshness, about my early years. The very look of me was enough to produce in others a sense of chill, and the more I realized this, the less accommodating did I become. I have never learned how to wear my clothes, how to choose a tie, or tie it when chosen. I have never in all my life known what it is to be unself-conscious, or to laugh or play the fool. I cannot imagine myself forming one of a party on the "spree." I am by nature one of Nature's wet blankets. At the same time, I am cursed with an excess of sensitiveness, and I was never able to stand being laughed at, no matter how good-humored the laughter might be. On the other hand, whenever I made a joke at other people's expense, I always, without meaning to, struck so savagely that my victims never forgave me. I invariably chose to make fun of the one thing, some physical infirmity, for instance, about which I ought to have kept silent. Because of my shyness, and because of my pride, I adopted to women that superior attitude of the hectoring schoolmaster, which, of all things, they most resent. I never noticed what they were wearing. The more conscious I was of their dislike, the more intolerable did I become. My youth was a prolonged condition of suicide. I was deliberately uncouth simply because I was afraid of being unconsciously so.

Rightly or wrongly, I blamed my mother for this temperament of mine. I had got the idea that I was paying for the fact that, ever since my childhood, I had been cosseted, supervised, and looked after far too much. I was abominably brutal to her at this time. She doted on me, as I have said, to a ridiculous extent. I could not forgive her for lavishing on me the affection that I was fated to have from nobody else. You must forgive me for harping on this subject. Only the thought of what she gave makes it possible for me to endure that failure to give that has always marked your attitude to me. It is right and proper that I should pay the price of my misdeeds. She has been dead now, poor woman, for many years, and the memory of her lives only in the heart of an old and worn-out man. How terribly she would have suffered could she have foreseen how the future was to avenge her!

Yes, I was a brute. In the little dining room at the cottage, under the hanging lamp at mealtimes, I would answer her timid questions with the barest monosyllables or would fly into sullen rages on the slightest excuse, and often on no excuse at all.

She made no attempt to understand, never tried to discover the reasons for my outbursts of temper, but submitted to them as to the whim of some angry god. It was because I had been ill, she said: I must learn to relax. And then she would go on to explain that she was too ignorant ever to hope to be able to understand me. "I realize that an old woman is no fit companion for a boy of your age. . . ." In the past she had been careful, not to say miserly, about money, but now she gave me far more than I asked for, encouraged me to spend lavishly, and used to bring me back from Bordeaux the most ridiculous ties, which I obstinately refused to wear.

We made friends with some neighbors, to whose daughter I proceeded to lay siege—though I did not care two pins about her. She had been ill and was spending a winter of convalescence at Arcachon. My mother was terribly worried. She was afraid I might catch something from her or compromise her by my attentions and be jockeyed into an engagement. I realize now that I went on with my courtship (which, as it happened, was entirely without effect) simply and solely with the intention of hurting her.

We returned to Bordeaux after a year's absence. We had moved. My mother had bought a house on one of the boulevards but had said nothing to me about it because she wanted to spring it upon me as a surprise. I was staggered when the front door was opened by a manservant. The whole of the first floor was reserved for my especial use. Everything looked brand-new. I was secretly dazzled by a luxury that, looking back, I now see must have been pretty awful. But I kept my pleasure to myself and, such was my cruelty, spoke to her only in disparagement of her efforts and nagged at her about the expense.

It was then that she gave me a triumphant account of her stewardship—though there was absolutely no need for her to do so, since most of the money came from her side of the family. An income of fifty thousand francs, to say nothing of what the timber brought in, constituted at that time, and especially in the provinces, a very "tidy" fortune. Any other young man would have used it to make a career for himself and to buy his right of entry into the highest ranks of local society. In my case, it was not ambition that was lacking, but the dislike that I felt for my companions in law school and concealed with difficulty.

Most of them were the sons of leading families in the city and had been educated by the Jesuits. As a mere secondary-school product, and the grandson of a shepherd, I could not forgive them for the hateful sense of envy that their manners roused in me, though I regarded them as my intellectual inferiors. Envy of those whom one despises is a degrading passion and may well poison a whole life.

But I did envy them, and I did despise them, while their contempt of me (probably the product of my imagination) served to exacerbate my resentment. To a youth of my temperament it never even occurred to try to win their friendship. In fact, I did all I could to make common cause with their adversaries. That hatred of religion, which, for so long, has been my dominant passion, which has caused you so much suffering and has set a wall of enmity between us, started in law school in 1879 and 1880 when Article 7 was voted by the chamber. It was the year that saw the famous decrees and the expulsion of the Jesuits.

Until that time I had been indifferent to such matters. My mother never talked to me about religion, except to say—"I am quite easy in my mind: if people like ourselves are not saved, then nobody will be." She had me baptized. My first communion, which I took while at school, left on me the impression merely of a boring formality, and my memory of it is extremely vague. In any case, it was unique. I never took communion again. My ignorance in all matters touching religion was profound. When, as a child, I used to pass priests in the street, I always thought of them as of people wearing a disguise, as a species of maskers. I never grappled with problems of faith, and when, later, I came up against them, I approached them only from the political angle.

I founded a study circle that used to meet at the Café Voltaire. Its value to me was that of a training ground in public speaking. The boy who was so shy in his personal dealings with others became a totally different person in open debate. I had a number of followers, and thoroughly enjoyed the feeling that I was their leader, but this did not prevent me from despising them, just as I despised the middle-class youths among my fellow students. I resented the simpleminded way in which they exhibited their petty motives, because it forced me to realize that my own motives were precisely similar. They were the sons of minor civil servants, former scholarship boys, intelligent, ambitious, but embittered. There was no affection in the flattery they offered me. I asked them to dinner once or twice, and those evenings were for them red-letter occasions, much talked about. But their manners disgusted me, and a time came when I could no longer resist the temptation to make fun of them. They were mortally offended and never forgot.

Nevertheless, my hatred of religion, and of all that had to do with it, was perfectly sincere. My social conscience was beginning to give me trouble. I made my mother pull down the wattle-and-daub cottages in which our farmhands lived on an insufficient diet of thin wine and black bread. For the first time in her life she tried to stand up to me: "You'll get no thanks for it. . . ."

I did not press the point. I knew only too well that my adversaries and I had the same ruling passion—land and money—and I hated having to admit it. There are, in all societies, the "haves" and the "have-nots," and I realized that I should always belong to the "haves." My fortune was as large as, if not larger than, that of the solemn asses who, I thought, averted their eyes when they saw me, but would be only too glad to take my hand if I should offer it. There was no lack of those, both of the Right and of the Left, who were delighted at a chance of throwing my two thousand hectares of timber and vineyard in my teeth on the public platform.

You must forgive me for dwelling on this subject. It is essential that you should have a thorough grasp of these details if you are to understand what our meeting meant to the sort of disgruntled creature I had become, and what wonderful hopes I built on our mutual love. That I, the son of peasants, whose mother had gone about with her head tied up in a handkerchief, should actually marry into the Fondaudège family, was something at which the imagination boggled. It was beyond my power to conceive.

III

I broke off in my writing because the light was getting bad and because I could hear voices below. Not that any of you were making much noise. Far from it, you were being particularly careful to keep your voices down, and that was what worried me. Formerly, I could always overhear your conversations from this room, but now you have grown suspicious and have taken to whispering. You told me the other day that I was getting "hard of hearing," but that is not true. I can catch the sound of trains rumbling over the viaduct perfectly well. No, I certainly am not deaf. The truth of the matter is that you are all of you talking in low voices. You want to make quite certain that I shall not know what you are talking about. What is it that you want to keep from me? Business worries? There they all are, hanging round you, on the lookout for what they can pick up—our son-in-law in the rum trade, and our grandson-in-law who does nothing, and our son, Hubert, the stockbroker . . . the chap who pays 20 percent and has everybody's money to play with!

Don't rely on me: I'm not shelling out! "It would be so easy"—you'll murmur to me tonight—"to fell some of the pines." You will remind me that Hubert's two girls have been living with their parents-in-law since their marriage because they can't afford to furnish homes of their own. "We've got masses of stuff just rotting away in the loft: it wouldn't cost us anything to lend them some of it. . . ." That's the suggestion you'll be making to me in an hour or so. "They resent our attitude. They never come to see us. I'm being cheated out of my own grandchildren. . . ." That's what you've all been whispering about so busily.

I've been reading over the stuff I wrote yesterday evening. I must have been suffering from a sort of delirium. How could I so let my feelings get the better of me? I started this as a letter, but it's a letter no longer. It has become a diary, now and then broken off, now and then resumed. . . . Shall I tear it up and begin all over again? No, I can't do that: time is pressing. What I have written I have written. After all, didn't I want to make a clean breast to you of everything?—didn't I want to force you to look into the bottom of my mind? For thirty years I have been nothing to you but a machine for dealing out thousand-franc notes, a machine that has been running badly, a machine that you've got to patch up until the happy day when you'll be able to break it open, empty it, and plunge your hands into the treasure it contains.

There, I'm letting my temper run away with me again. I'm back at the point where I left off. I must trace this evil mood of mine to its source, must recall that fatal night. . . . But first of all, I would have you cast your mind back to the occasion of our first meeting.

In August 1883 I was staying with my mother at Luchon. At that time the Hotel Sacarron was crammed with heavily upholstered furniture, cushions, and stuffed chamoix. After all these years, it is the limes of the Allées d'Ettigny that I smell when the season comes round for the limes to flower. The patter of mules, the tinkling of bells, the crack of whips used to wake me in the mornings. The water of the mountain torrents gurgled in the streets. The air was full of voices calling croissants and milk loaves. Guides rode by on horseback. I used to watch the parties of climbers setting out.

The whole of the first floor was occupied by the Fondaudège family. They had King Leopold's suite. "They must be making the money fly!" said my mother. But that didn't prevent them from being always in arrears when it came to settling their business debts (they had taken a lease of a big plot of land that we owned in the docks, for purposes connected with their shipping interests).

My mother and I always dined at the *table d'hôte,* but you and your family had meals served to you separately. I can still

remember that round table in the window, and your fat grandmother who concealed her baldness under an arrangement of
black lace with quivering jet ornaments. I felt convinced that
she was smiling at me, but it was the way her tiny eyes were set
in her face, and her great slit of a mouth, that produced that
impression. A nun waited on her, a woman with a puffy, bilious
face swathed in starched linen. How beautiful your mother
was! She wore nothing but black, being in perpetual mourning
for the two children she had lost. It was she, not you, who was
the first object of my furtive admiration. The nakedness of her
throat, her arms, and her hands set my heart beating. She wore
no jewelry. I played with the idea of stalking her à la Stendhal
and gave myself until the evening to murmur a word to her or
to slip a note into her hand. You I scarcely noticed. I had an
idea that young girls did not interest me. Besides, you had that
particular arrogance that takes the form of never looking at
other people and is tantamount to denying their existence.

One day, on my way back from the casino, I came on my
mother in conversation with Madame Fondaudège. The latter's
manner was obsequious and just a little too friendly. She gave
me the impression of somebody who knows that it is useless to
try to lower herself to the level of her companion. Mother, on
the other hand, was speaking in a loud voice. She was dealing
with a tenant, and, in her eyes, a Fondaudège was no more
than a debtor in arrears. A countrywoman by nature, and an

owner of land, she had a profound distrust of big business and of the kind of fortunes it produced, none of them built on a foundation of solid property. I broke in on the discussion just as she was saying: "Of course I have complete confidence in Monsieur Fondaudège's signature: all the same—"

For the first time in my life I intervened in a business argument. Madame Fondaudège got the extension she wanted. I have often thought, since then, that my mother's peasant shrewdness did not mislead her. Your family has cost me a pretty penny, and if I had just sat back and let myself be sucked dry, your son, your daughter, and your grandson-in-law would very soon have made ducks and drakes of my fortune and swallowed it up in their business speculations. Business indeed!—what has it ever amounted to?—a ground-floor office, a telephone, and a typist! . . . Behind that setting the money has been drained away by the bucketful. . . . But I anticipate: we are still in 1883 at Bagnères-de-Luchon.

That powerful family of yours was now all smiles. Your grandmother went on talking the whole time because she was deaf. No sooner did I have an opportunity of chatting with your mother after dinner than I found that she bored me and completely upset all my preconceived romantic ideas. You will, I am sure, forgive me if I point out that her conversation was tedious in the extreme. So limited was the world in which she lived, and so jejune was her vocabulary that, after the first few minutes, I had had enough and was at my wits' end to keep the talk going at all.

My attention, thus diverted from the mother, became fixed upon the daughter. I failed, at first, to notice the suspicious absence of all obstacles to our intimacy. But then, why should it have occurred to me that your family might be congratulating themselves on having made a good "catch"? I remember one drive, in particular, up the valley of the Lys. Your grandmother and her nun were in the back of the victoria: you and I occupied the little let-down seats facing them. God knows there were carriages and to spare in Luchon! Only the Fondaudèges would have dreamed of bringing their own!

The horses proceeded at a walking pace, moving in a cloud of flies. The good sister's face was shiny, and her eyes half shut. Your grandmother sat flapping a fan that she had bought in the Allées d'Ettigny. It was decorated with a picture of a matador giving the coup de grâce to a black bull. You had long gloves, in spite of the heat. Everything you wore was white, down to your high-laced boots. Ever since the death of your two brothers, you said, you had had "a devotion to white." I did not know what "having a devotion to white" meant. I have learned since what a point your family made of these rather exotic "devotions." In my then state of mind I thought it all rather poetical. How can I possibly make you understand the emotion that you roused in me? I had become suddenly aware that I was no longer unpleasing, had ceased to repel, was not odious anymore. One of the most important moments of my life was when you said: "How extraordinary that a man should have such long lashes!"

I was careful to keep my advanced ideas dark. I remember how, in the course of that drive, we got out in order to lighten the carriage on a hill, how your grandmother and her nun told their beads, and how the old coachman, long trained in the way he should go, made his responses to their Ave Marias. You looked at me with a smile, but I remained solemn. It cost me nothing to accompany you to eleven o'clock Mass on Sundays. There was, for me, no metaphysical idea attached to the ceremony. It was merely the religious exercise of a class in which I was proud to find myself numbered, a species of ancestor worship adapted to the use of the bourgeoisie, a hotchpotch of rites with nothing but a social significance. Occasionally you would give me a sidelong glance, and the memory of those Masses remains associated in my mind with the staggering discovery, which I made at that time, that I was capable of arousing interest, pleasure, and emotion in another. The love that I felt was all mixed up with the love that I inspired—or thought I inspired. There was nothing real about my own feelings. What counted for me was my belief in the love that *you* felt. I caught my reflection in the mirror of somebody else's personality, and in the image thus presented there was nothing repulsive. In that blissful state of relaxation I blossomed and flowered. I remember how I thawed in the warmth of your gaze, how emotion gushed from the opened freshets of my being. The most ordinary expressions of affection—the pressure of a hand, a flower laid between the pages of a book—were wholly new to me, and I succumbed to their enchantment.

The only person who did not benefit from this change in me was my mother. I felt that she was hostile to the dream (the lunatic dream, I thought) that was forming in my mind. I resented the fact that she was not dazzled. "Can't you see," she kept on saying, "that these people are trying to land you?" It never occurred to her that by talking like that she might well destroy the immense happiness I was feeling just because, for the first time, I believed that I had found favor in a young woman's eyes. There was at least one woman in the world, I told myself, who found me attractive, who might actually entertain the idea of marrying me. For that was what I believed, in spite of my mother's skepticism. You were too great and powerful as a family (so ran my silent argument) to find any advantage in a marriage with such as me. Nevertheless, I regarded my mother almost with hatred for throwing even a shadow of doubt on the reality of my bliss.

She went her own way and set about finding out what she could. The sources of her intelligence were the leading banks.

It was a great day for me when she had to admit that the House of Fondaudège, in spite of occasional difficulties, still enjoyed a high reputation. "Their profits are fantastic, but they are living at too high a rate," she said. "Everything goes on horses and liveried servants. They are more intent on cutting a dash than on putting money by."

This verdict of the banks set the seal upon my happiness. The disinterestedness of your family was proved. Your people were smiling on my suit because they liked me. It seemed to me, suddenly, the most natural thing in the world that I should be generally liked. I was allowed to walk alone with you, of an evening, in the casino gardens. How strange it is that when life is just beginning for us, and when a little happiness comes our way, no warning voice is heard. "However long your life, you will never know any bliss comparable to these few hours. Drink them to the dregs, because Fate holds nothing more in store for you. This first gushing of cool water is also the last. Quench your thirst once and for all, for you will never again have an opportunity to drink." If only someone had said that!

For I was convinced, on the contrary, that a long life of passionate happiness was opening out before me. I set too little store on the evenings that we spent together, motionless, under the sleeping trees.

❊

Signs there were, however, though I failed to interpret them aright. Do you remember one night in particular, when we were sitting on a bench by the winding path that climbs the hill behind the hot baths? All of a sudden you started to sob. The fragrance of your wet cheeks comes back to me still, as of an unknown sorrow. I thought your tears were those of happy love. I was too young to know the meaning of that choking misery. True, you hid it from me. "It's nothing," you said: "it's just being here with you."

You were not lying to me, liar though you are. It was, indeed, because I was with you that you cried, with me; and not with someone else, with that other whose name, at long last, you told me in this very room where I sit writing now, an old man near his death, surrounded by a battery of eager eyes strained for the coming kill.

There, on that bench by the winding path at Superbagnères, we sat. My face was pressed against your neck, your shoulder, and in my nostrils was the scent of a very young girl in tears. It was mingled with the scent of wet leaves and of mint in the warm, moist Pyrenean night. The branches of the lime trees round the bandstand on the Place des Thermes below us caught the glint of lamps. An old Englishman from the hotel was catching the moths that fluttered round them in a long-handled net. "Lend me your handkerchief," you said. I wiped away your tears and treasured the handkerchief against my heart.

I need say no more than that I had become a different person. There was a radiance in my face—I knew it from the way the women looked at me. Those evening tears brought no suspicion in their train.

Besides, for one night such as that there were many when you were all happiness, when you leaned on me and clung to my arm. I walked too quickly for you, and your efforts to keep up with me made you out of breath.

I was, as a lover, very self-controlled. You appealed to some part of me that was untouched, unspoiled. Never once was I tempted to abuse the confidence that your parents placed in me. I did not so much as dream that their attitude might be the result of cold calculation.

I was a changed being, so completely changed that one day—it's only now, after forty years, that I can pluck up sufficient courage to make this confession. It won't, I think, when you read this letter, give you much cause to feel triumphant. Here it is. One day, when we were driving through the Lys Valley, we got out of the victoria. The streams were gurgling. I was rubbing a leaf of fennel between my fingers. The lower slopes of the mountains were growing dark, but the light was still secure upon their peaks. . . . An intense feeling suddenly came over me, an almost physical certainty that another world *did* exist, a reality of which we know only the shadow.

That feeling lasted for a moment only. In the course of a long and miserable life I have had comparable experiences, but only at wide intervals. The very strangeness of what happened to me then gave it an enhanced value in my eyes. That is why, in our terrible religious squabbles of a later date, I had to keep the memory of it from my mind. I owe it to you to make this admission. But the time has not yet come for me to embark upon that subject.

There is no point in my recalling our engagement. The whole thing was settled one evening. It happened without my meaning it to. I rather think that you interpreted something I said in a sense different from the one I intended. I found myself bound to you and was too staggered to protest. What is the use of going over all that old ground again? There was, however, one horrible incident that I still cannot get out of my mind.

There and then, on the spot, you made a condition. In what you called the "interests of harmony" you flatly refused to consider the idea of my mother living with us, or even of having her under the same roof. You and your parents had quite made up your minds. You wouldn't even discuss the matter.

How vividly, after all these years, I remember that stifling hotel room with its open window giving on to the Allées

d'Ettigny! Through the lowered venetian blind a golden pow-
dering of dust drifted in on us. In our ears was the cracking of
whips, the sound of a Tyrolean tune. My mother had a head-
ache and was lying on the sofa, dressed in a skirt and a petticoat
bodice (she had never in her life possessed a dressing gown, a
peignoir, or a wrap). She would, she said, give up the ground-
floor suite to us and make do with one room on the third floor.
I snatched at this opportunity and took the plunge.

"Isa thinks that it would be very much better . . ."—and
all the time I was talking I kept glancing furtively at her old
face and looking away again. She was crumpling the trimming
of her bodice between her gnarled fingers. If only she had put
up a fight I could have dealt with the situation, but her silence
made anger impossible.

She pretended not to be hurt or even surprised. When at
last she did speak she chose her words carefully, so as to lead
me to suppose that she had always known our separation to be
inevitable.

"I shall spend most of the year at Aurigne," she said: "it's
in better condition than the other farms, and you can have
Calèse. I'll have a little garden room run up at Aurigne. Three
rooms will be quite enough for me. It won't cost much, but it's
a nuisance, all the same, to incur even a small expense when I
may be dead by next year. But you'll find it will come in useful, later, for the duck shooting. It'll be pleasant living there in

October. I know you don't care much about shooting, but you may have children who will."

No ingratitude of mine could ever exhaust the treasures of her love. Driven from one position, it reformed its ranks elsewhere. It took what I left and made do. But that same evening you said:

"Is there anything wrong with your mother?"

Next day she looked just as usual. Your father arrived from Bordeaux with his eldest daughter and his son-in-law. Somebody must have told them what was going on. They looked me up and down. I could almost hear them comparing notes: "D'you think he'll do? That old mother of his is really the last straw. . . ." I shall never forget my surprise when I saw your sister, Marie-Thérèse—the one you called Marinette. She was older than you by a year but looked younger, with her slim body, her long neck, the great coil of hair that looked too heavy for her, and those childlike eyes. The old man to whom your father had sold her, Baron Philipot, gave me the horrors. But since his death I have often thought that that sexagenarian was one of the unhappiest men I have ever come across. What tortures the poor fool must have suffered in his efforts to make his young wife forget that he was old! He was so tightly buckled into his stays that he could scarcely breathe. His high, wide, starched collar scarified his jowl and his dewlaps. The refulgence of his dyed moustache and whiskers merely accentuated the purple ruin of his face. He scarcely listened when anyone spoke to him, was always looking round for a mirror, and, when he found one, how we laughed (do you remember?) at the way the old idiot mopped and mowed at his reflection and could never keep his eyes off himself! He was incapable of smiling, because of his false teeth. By an exercise of willpower—which never failed—he kept his mouth perpetually shut. We used to notice, too, the peculiar way in which he put on his hat so as not to disarrange the extraordinary lock of hair that started from the nape of his neck and spread out over his skull like the delta of a half-dried-up river.

Your father, who was his contemporary, was still attractive to women, in spite of his white beard, his baldness, and his paunch. Even in business matters he laid himself out to exert his charm. My mother was the only person who stood out against him. Maybe the blow I had just dealt her had had a hardening effect. She argued every clause of the marriage contract as though it had been a deed of sale or a lease. I pretended to be indignant at her demands—though I was secretly overjoyed to think that my interests were in such good hands. If, today, my fortune is entirely separate from yours, if you have so little hold on me, I owe it all to my mother who insisted on the most rigorous form of settlement and behaved as though I were a daughter who had made up her mind to marry a debauchee.

As soon as it became clear that the Fondaudège family was not going to use these demands as an excuse for breaking off the engagement, I was able to sleep calmly in my bed. They put up with me—or so I thought—because you had set your heart on having me as a husband.

Mamma would not hear of an "allowance," but insisted that your dowry should be paid down in cash. "They keep on quoting Baron Philipot as a precedent," she said: "apparently, he took the eldest without a sou . . . and so I should think! They must have got a pretty return from handing over the poor child to that nasty old man! But with us, the shoe's on the other foot. They thought I should be dazzled at the prospect of marrying my son into their precious family. That shows how little they know me!"

We two, the "turtledoves," made a great show of not being interested in the discussion. I imagine that you felt no less confidence in the genius of your father than I did in that of my mother. As a matter of fact, I suspect that neither of us quite realized what a store we both of us set by money.

No, that's unfair. You've never been fond of money except for the children's sake. No doubt you'd gladly have murdered me if, by doing so, you could have made them richer. But, then, you'd have gladly given them the bread out of your own mouth.

I, on the other hand, adore money, and I don't mind admitting it. It gives me a sense of security. So long as I remain in control of my fortune, you have no weapon against me. "At our age one needs so little"—that is your constant refrain; but how wrong you are! An old man lives only by virtue of what he possesses. As soon as he's got nothing, out he goes on the scrap heap. For us the only choice is between the almshouse, the workhouse, and a private fortune. One is always hearing of peasants who let their old parents starve to death after they have stripped them of everything. The same holds good, as I know from experience, though with rather more form and ceremony, of the middle classes. Yes, I *am* afraid of being poor. I have the feeling that I can never pile up enough gold. You want it because it attracts you. I want it because it is my only protection.

The hour of the Angelus has gone by, and I did not hear the bell. . . . But, of course, it wouldn't have been rung today because it's Good Friday. The men of the family are arriving tonight by car. I shall come down to dinner. I want to see the whole gang. I feel much stronger when they're all ranged against me than I do when they tackle me separately. And there's another reason. I like making a point of eating my cutlet on this day of penitence—not out of bravado, but just to show you that I have kept my willpower intact, that I am not prepared to yield on a single point.

All the positions that I have occupied for the last forty-five years, and from which you have failed to dislodge me, would fall one by one if I made the least concession. With the rest of

the family fasting on beans and salt fish, my Good Friday cutlet will serve as a sign that you don't stand a chance of skinning
me so long as there is breath in my body.

IV

You see, I wasn't wrong. My presence among you yesterday evening completely upset your plans. Only the children, sitting apart at their own table, were happy, because on Good Friday they have chocolate and bread-and-butter for supper. I must say I find it difficult to tell who's who among them. Janine, who's my granddaughter, has a child of her own old enough to walk. . . . I let everyone see that there was nothing wrong with my appetite. So that the children shouldn't get any false ideas about my cutlet, you had told them that the state of my health and my great age made it necessary. . . . What really did terrify me was Hubert's optimism. He said he felt confident that the market would show an upward trend soon—but with the air of a man for whom that hypothetical trend was a matter of life and death. I can never get over the fact that he's my son—but he is. Yes, this man of forty's my son. My reason admits it, but not my imagination. For some curious reason I can't face it. And suppose things do go wrong for him? After all, a stockbroker who offers such high dividends plays high and takes

big risks. . . . One of these days I shall be told that the family
honor is in jeopardy. . . . The family honor, indeed! That's an
idol before which I will *not* sacrifice. The sooner I make up
my mind on the point, the better. I've got to stand my ground
and not allow myself to get sentimental—more especially as
there is always that old Fondaudège uncle in the background
who'll play up even if I don't . . . But I'm digressing, going
off on a false scent, or, rather, I'm shirking the recollection of
that night when, though you did not realize it at the time, you
destroyed all our hopes of happiness.

It's odd to think that you've probably forgotten all about it.
A few hours in the warm dusk of this room decided our desti-
nies. Every word you spoke increased the distance between us,
and yet, you noticed nothing. Your memory, which is a junk
shop of a thousand trivialities, has retained not one single iota
of that disaster. You make a great to-do about believing in the
life everlasting, but you didn't seem to realize that what you
were gambling with at that moment, what you were endanger-
ing, was my immortal soul. The birth of love in my heart had
made me sensitive to the climate of faith and adoration that
was the ambience in which you lived. I loved you, and I loved
the spiritual elements in your being. When you knelt down in
your long, schoolgirl's nightgown, I felt deeply moved.

We occupied this room where I now sit writing. Why did
we come to Calèse, to my mother's, when we got back from the

honeymoon? (I had refused her offer of the place. It was her creation, and she loved it.) When, later, I sought out food for my rancor, I remembered a number of circumstances that had, at first, escaped me, or from which I had deliberately averted my gaze. In the first place, on the ground that an uncle once removed had just died, your family had insisted on keeping the wedding ceremony as quiet as possible. It was as plain as houses that they felt thoroughly ashamed of the connection. Baron Philipot had put it about that his young sister-in-law had fallen madly in love with a young man at Bagnères-de-Luchon, a charming enough fellow, with a future before him and plenty of money, but of doubtful birth. "Fact is," he said, "he doesn't belong." To hear him speak, you'd have thought I was somebody's bastard. On the whole, however, he thought my lack of family a good thing. At least there was no need to blush for my relations. All things considered, my old mother was quite presentable and seemed to know her place. According to him, you were a spoiled child who could twist her parents round her little finger, and my fortune had seemed big enough to persuade the Fondaudège clan to consent to the marriage while shutting their eyes to its many disadvantages.

When this tittle-tattle reached my ears it told me nothing, really, that I did not know already. I was so happy that I refused to attach any importance to it. Truth to tell, the almost secret way in which the wedding was carried through suited me very well—for how could I have possibly found groomsmen in the down-at-heels circle of which I was the center? Pride kept me from making advances to those who had so recently been my enemies, though my brilliant marriage would have made reconciliation easy. I have already, in the course of this confession, shown myself in such ugly colors that I may as well go further and make no effort to conceal this trait in me that may be described as independence of mind or inflexibility. I refuse to bow the knee to anybody, and I remain true to my ideas. In connection with this latter point, I may as well say that my marriage had given me a few twinges of conscience. I had promised your parents that I would do nothing that might alienate you from the practice of your religion, but I had in no way compromised my own freedom of action, except insofar as I had undertaken not to become a Freemason. As a matter of fact, you none of you thought of making any further demand on me. In those days the general view was that religion was the wife's affair. In your world, the husband—to use the accepted formula, "accompanied his wife to Mass." I had already, at Luchon, given you ample proof that I wasn't likely to kick at that.

When we returned from Venice in September '85, your parents made excuses for not receiving us in their château of Cenon, where, owing to the presence of their friends, and Philipot's, there was no room available. We found it convenient, therefore, to stay for a while with my mother. The memory of the brutal way in which we had treated her did not embarrass us in the least. We were perfectly prepared to live with her for as long as it suited us.

She was careful to give no outward sign of triumph. The house was ours, she said, and we were free to invite whom we liked: she would make herself scarce, and nobody need see her. "I know how to disappear," she added: "I spend almost all my time out of doors." This was true, for she gave much of her attention to the vines, the cellar, the chickens, and the laundry. After meals she went for a while to her own room and always apologized when she found us in the drawing room when she came down. She regularly knocked before coming in. I had to explain to her that she mustn't do that, that it wasn't "the thing." She even suggested that you should take over the house-keeping, but you did, at least, spare her that mortification. But that was only because you had no wish to saddle yourself with her duties. How terribly condescending you were to her, and what a humble gratitude she showed!

You did not come between her and me as much as she had feared you would. Actually, I was a great deal nicer to her than I had been before our marriage. Our mad fits of laughter were a never-ending cause of surprise to her. She could scarcely believe that the happy young husband whom she saw before her was the same person as the repressed, unyielding son she had formerly known. She explained the change by the fact that she hadn't known how to handle me. I had always been too far "above" her. You were repairing the damage that she had done.

I remember her admiration when she saw you daubing away at screens and tambourines, and when you sang or played—always breaking down in the same places—one of Mendelssohn's "Songs without Words" on the piano.

Young women friends sometimes came to see you. "You're going to meet my mother-in-law," you would tell them: "one of the genuine old ladies from the country. You don't come across many of them nowadays." You decided that she had what you called a "style of her own." She had got into the habit of speaking patois to the servants, and that, you thought, was very "smart." You even went so far as to show your visitors a daguerreotype of her at the age of fifteen, in which she appeared with her head tied up in a handkerchief. You were fond of quoting a saying about old peasant families having "more true distinction than many of noble rank. . . ." How very conventional you were in those days! It was motherhood that restored you to your natural self.

I keep shying away from the story of what happened that night. It was so hot that we had left the blinds up, in spite of your terror of bats. When the branches of a lime tree brushed against the house we knew precisely what it was, though the sound was exactly like that of someone breathing at the far end of the room. Sometimes the wind in the leaves was like the noise of rain. The waning moon lit up the floor and the pale phantoms of your scattered clothes. We no longer heard the murmurs of the meadow grass, so much had they become part of the general silence.

"We really must go to sleep," you said . . . but all the time a shadow roamed about our inert and weary bodies. Not alone did we struggle up from the depths: the unknown Rodolphe came with us. Each time I took you in my arms I woke the memory of him in your heart.

When I loosed you from my embrace, we felt his presence. I did not want to suffer: I was afraid of suffering. The instinct of self-preservation applies to happiness as to other forms of life. I knew I must not ask you any questions. I let his name burst like a bubble on the surface of our life. Beneath the waters there slept a principle of corruption, a putrid secret, and I did nothing to stir it from the mud. But you, wretched woman, felt the need to liberate in words the cheated passion that still hungered for satisfaction. One question of mine sufficed to bring it into the open. "Who, precisely, was this fellow Rodolphe?" "I'm afraid there's a lot I ought to have told you—oh, nothing really serious, don't worry."

You spoke hurriedly and in a low voice. Your head no longer lay against my shoulder. Already the tiny space that separated our stretched bodies had become unbridgeable.

He was the son of some Austrian woman and of a big industrialist from the north. . . . You had met him at Aix when you had been there with your grandmother the year before we had got to know one another at Luchon. He had just left Cambridge. You made no attempt to describe him, but I knew that he possessed all the graces that I felt myself to lack. The moonlight on the sheet illuminated my coarse peasant hands with their spatulate fingers. You had done nothing "wrong," though he was, you said, less respectful than I had been. My recollection of what you confessed is vague: not that it mattered. *That* wasn't what worried me. If you had been genuinely in love with him, I could have forgiven one of those short, sharp surrenders in which the innocence of childhood melts into nothingness. But my mind was already full of questions. "How could she have fallen in love with me scarcely twelve months after so great a passion?" I felt frozen by terror. "It was all a sham," I told myself: "she lied to me. That liberating influence was all a make-believe. How could I have been such a fool as to fancy that a young girl could love me—me whom nobody could love?"

The stars of the night's end were twinkling. A blackbird woke. The breeze, which we could hear among the leaves, even before we felt it on our bodies, filled the curtains and brought refreshment to my eyes as in the days when I was happy. Only ten minutes before, that happiness had been real to me, and now I was thinking about the "time when I was happy." I asked another question:

"Was it that he didn't want you?" You felt the sting of that. I can still hear the special voice you put on when your vanity was touched. On the contrary, you said, he had been madly in love and very proud at the thought of marrying a Fondaudège. The trouble was that it had come to the ears of his parents that you had lost two brothers from consumption before they were grown up. In view of the fact that he, too, suffered from delicate health, they wouldn't hear of the match.

I asked my questions very calmly. No words of mine could possibly have given you any idea of what it was you were so busily pulling to bits.

"Actually, darling," you said, "it was quite providential for us, the way things turned out. You know how proud my parents are—rather absurdly so, I must admit. It was their obsession about this marriage that never came off that made our happiness—mine and yours—possible. You must have noticed the importance that people in my little world attach to health where marriage is concerned. Mamma got it firmly fixed in her head that the whole town knew what had happened and that no one would ever want to marry me. She was quite convinced that I should die an old maid. I can't tell you the life she led me—oh, for months and months—as though I hadn't enough troubles of my own! . . . In the end she persuaded us, both Papa and me, that I was out of the marriage market for good!"

I carefully refrained from saying anything that might have made you suspicious. You repeated what you had said before, that the whole thing had been providential.

"I fell in love with you from the moment we met. We had said many, many prayers at Lourdes before going to Luchon, and as soon as I set eyes on you I knew that they had been answered."

You were far from guessing how those words grated on my nerves. Those who oppose you in religion have, really, a very much nobler idea of it than you realize, or than they realize themselves. Why, otherwise, should they be so affronted at the way in which you debase it? Can you honestly think it right and proper to ask for tangible rewards from the God whom you call your Father? . . . But that's beside the point, which was, quite simply, that you'd all pounced hungrily on the first snail that popped its head out of its shell. After hearing what you had said I could have no doubt of that.

How monstrous a thing our marriage was I realized only at that moment. Before it could take place at all your mother had had to have a brainstorm and infect both you and your father with her own temporary lunacy. . . . You told me that the Philipots had gone so far as to threaten to disown you should you marry me. Actually, at Luchon, while we were all laughing at the old fool, he was doing all he could to persuade your family to break it all off.

"But I stuck to you, darling, and he got nothing for his pains."

Again and again you told me that you had no regrets. I let you talk and saved my breath. You could never, you assured me, have been happy with the precious Rodolphe. He was too good-looking. Love, for him, meant not giving but taking. The first woman who tried could have got him away from you.

You were blissfully unaware that your voice changed whenever you mentioned him—lost some of its sharpness and became tremulous, with a sort of a cooing sound in it, as though old sighs, treasured within your breast, found freedom when his name was spoken.

He could never have made you happy because he was handsome, charming, and beloved! The logical deduction from that was that I could be the joy of your life because I was nothing much to look at and put people off with my surly manners! I gathered from your description that he had the intolerable arrogance of all young Frenchmen who have been to Cambridge and learned to ape the English. . . . Would you really rather have had a husband who couldn't choose a suit or tie a tie, who hated games and was incapable of the sophisticated frivolity that consists in avoiding all serious subjects, in shying away from emotional entanglements or any show of feeling, and in living with carefree elegance? You had accepted the inferior me (so I was to believe) merely because I happened to have swum into your ken just when your mother, afflicted by her change of life, had convinced herself that you would never find a husband, because you would not, or could not, remain unmarried a moment longer, and because I happened to have enough money to provide an excuse in the eyes of the world. . . .

I did my best to control my breathing. I clenched my fists, I bit my lips. Many times since then I have felt such a loathing of myself that I have turned with revulsion from the very thought of my body and of my feelings, and always, in such moments, my thoughts have gone back to the young man of 1885, the husband of twenty-three, sitting with his arms tightly crossed in a frenzied attempt to stifle his young love.

I shivered. You noticed it and broke off in the middle of what you were saying:

"Are you cold, Louis?"

"It was nothing," I said: "just a touch of gooseflesh."

"You're not going to tell me you're jealous?—that would really be too ridiculous!"

I swore to you that I did not feel the least twinge of jealousy—and it was true. How could I possibly have made you understand that my personal drama was something far beyond mere jealousy?

You were worried by my silence, but you had not the least idea how deeply I had been wounded. Your hand felt for mine in the darkness; you stroked my face. Your fingers felt no trace of tears, but perhaps the rigidity of my clenched jaws struck you as strange. You took fright. In your effort to light a candle you were lying half across me. The match wouldn't strike. I lay there half stifled under the weight of your hateful body.

"What's the matter with you? Don't lie there saying nothing! You're frightening me!"

I pretended to be surprised. I assured you that there was nothing to be frightened about.

"How silly of you, darling, to give me such a shock! . . . I'm going to put out the light and try to get some sleep."

You said no more. I watched the new day come, the day that would mark the beginning of a new life for me. The swallows were twittering under the eaves. A man crossed the yard, dragging his clogs. All I heard then I can hear still, after forty-five years—cocks crowing, bells ringing, a goods train on the viaduct. All I smelled then I can smell still—the scent that I love above all scents, of ashes carried by the wind from heath fires by the sea.

Suddenly I started up:

"Isa, that night you cried when we were sitting on a bench by the winding path at Superbagnères—was it because of him?"

You didn't say anything. I gripped your arm, but you shook yourself free with a sort of animal snarl and rolled over on your side. Your long hair was all about you as you slept. You lay curled up like some wild young creature of the woods, the blankets piled higgledy-piggledy on your body because of the dawn chill. What should I have gained by rousing you from your childlike slumbers? I knew already what I needed to know without hearing it from your lips.

I got up quietly and padded across on bare feet to the wardrobe mirror. I stared at myself as though I had been a stranger or, rather, as though I had suddenly become myself again—the man whom nobody loved, on whose account no one in the world had ever had a moment's suffering. I was filled with self-pity, thinking of my youth. I passed a great peasant hand across my unshaven cheeks, which were already showing dark beneath a harsh growth of beard with red lights in it.

I dressed in silence and went down to the garden. Mamma was in the rose walk. She always got up before the servants so as to air the house.

She spoke to me:

"Enjoying the cool of the day?"

Then, pointing to the mists on the lowland:

"It's going to be a scorcher. I must have every shutter closed by eight."

I kissed her with more show of affection than usual. She murmured, very low . . . "Dear boy. . . ." My heart (do you find it odd that I should speak of my heart?) felt ready to burst. A few hesitating words came to my lips . . . but how should I begin what I had to say? . . . would she understand? . . . Invariably I yield to the temptation of silence.

I walked down to the terrace. The young fruit trees were showing shadowy above the vines. The shoulder of the hill was thrusting the mist aside, breaking it into wisps and shreds. A belfry emerged from the thin fog, then the church to which it belonged, like a living body. It has always been your fixed opinion that churches, and all they stand for, leave me cold . . . let me tell you, then, what I felt at that moment. I felt that a man whose heart is broken as mine had been broken may be impelled to seek the reason for, the meaning of, his undoing: that, possibly, what has happened to him may conceal some significant secret, that what happens—especially in the world of the feelings—may, perhaps, carry a message the meaning of which he must interpret. . . . So, you see, there have been moments in my life when I have been capable of glimpsing things that might, perhaps, have drawn us together. . . .

But on that particular morning my emotion lasted for only a few moments. I still have a picture of myself going back toward the house. It was not yet eight o'clock, and already the sun was hot. You were leaning from your window, holding your hair in one hand, while, with the other, you brushed it. You did not see me. I stood still for a few seconds, looking up at you. I had been caught by a sudden spasm of hatred. After all these years, I can still taste its bitterness.

I ran to my desk and opened the drawer that I kept always locked. From it I took a little crumpled handkerchief, the same that you had used to wipe away your tears one evening at Superbagnères. I, poor fool, had pressed it to my heart. I took it now; I tied a stone to it as I might have done to a puppy I meant to drown, and threw it into the pond, which local country people call the "gutter."

V

Then began that era of the Great Silence, which has scarcely been broken for forty years. There was no outward sign of collapse. All went on as in the days of my happiness. We remained united in the flesh, but no ghost of Rodolphe was now born of our embrace, nor did you ever mention the dreadful name. At your bidding he had come, had prowled about our bed, had accomplished his work of destruction. All he could do now was to remain silent and await the long sequence of events, the delayed working of cause and effect.

You may, perhaps, have felt that you had done wrong to speak at all. It was not that you expected anything very serious to occur as a result of your admission. Still, it might have been wiser to keep his name out of our talk. I don't know whether you noticed that we no longer indulged in nightly chats. Those interminable discussions of ours were now a thing of the past. Whatever we said to one another we said only after due and careful thought. We were, each of us, on the defensive.

I used to start awake in the middle of the night. It was pain that woke me. I was fastened to you like a fox to the trap. Sometimes I tried to imagine what might have been said between us had I shaken you roughly, had I thrown you out of bed. "You're wrong"—you might have cried: "I didn't lie, and for the very good reason that I was in love with you."—"Yes, at second best, because it's always easy to consent to the physical act—which means nothing—in order to make your partner believe that you love him. I was no monster: any young girl who had truly loved me could have done with me what she would. . . ." Sometimes I groaned in the darkness, but you never woke.

Your first pregnancy made all attempts at explanation useless. Little by little it changed the nature of our relationship. It began before the time of the grape harvest. We went back to town. You had a miscarriage, as a result of which you were in bed for several weeks. By the following spring you were again with child. I had to take great care of you. Then began that long series of pregnancies, mishaps, and childbed, which gave me more pretexts than I needed for keeping away from you. I plunged into a secret life of debauchery—very secret, for I was beginning to appear more and more frequently in court—was "feeling my feet," as Mamma said—and had to be careful about my reputation. I had my special times, my regular habits. The man who would live an irregular life in the country has to develop the cunning of the hunted hare. Don't be afraid, Isa, I shall spare you all details of what, I know, fills you with horror. You may rest assured that I shall paint no picture here of the hell into which I descended almost every day. It was you, once, who had fished me out: it was you, now, who threw me back again.

Even had I been less prudent, you wouldn't have twigged a thing. After the birth of Hubert, you came out in your true colors. You were a mother, and nothing but a mother. You no longer paid the slightest attention to me. You didn't even notice my existence. It is quite literally true that you had eyes only for your young. In sowing the necessary seed, I had done all you wanted of me.

So long as the children were in the grub stage and did not interest me, there was no cause for quarrel between us. We never met except to perform those ritual acts that the body carries through as a matter of habit, and in which the man and the woman are, each, a thousand miles removed from their own flesh.

You began to take notice of me only when I, in my turn, started to prowl around our young family. You began to hate me only when I claimed my rights in them. It was not paternal instinct that dictated my attitude. I can bring myself now to make that admission, and you ought to be very grateful to me for doing so. I very soon became jealous of the passion that had waked in you. I tried to entice the children away for the sole purpose of punishing you. I deceived myself with any number of high-sounding reasons—duty, for instance, and my refusal to let a bigoted woman stunt young minds. But those were just excuses!

Shall I ever come to the end of my story? I began it for you, and already I feel it to be in the highest degree unlikely that you will be able to bear with it much longer. It is, fundamentally, for myself that I am writing. True to my character of an old barrister, I want to get my brief sorted out, to docket and arrange the various exhibits in that lost cause—my life. . . . Oh, those bells!—of course, tomorrow's Easter. I shall join you all downstairs in honor of the sacred feast—as I promised I would. "The children are always complaining that they never see you"—that's what you said to me this morning. Geneviève was standing beside you, close to my bed. She had something she wanted to ask me. I had heard you whispering together in the passage: "It'll be much better if you speak first . . ."—you said to her . . . I suppose it's something to do with her son-in-law, that blackguard, Phili. How cleverly I kept her from bringing him into the conversation or mentioning what it was that she was after! She left the room without having managed even to broach the subject. I know perfectly well what it's all about. I overheard your conversation the other evening. The drawing-room window is just below mine, and, when it's open, I only have to lean forward a little. She wants me to advance

Phili the capital he needs to buy a quarter share in a broker's firm. . . . It'd be as good an investment as any other. . . . Oh yes, I know all about that. . . . As though I hadn't seen the storm blowing up, as though I didn't know it was time now to tuck one's money away in a safe place! . . . If only they knew how much I made last month by anticipating the slump!

They've all gone to Vespers. Easter has emptied the house and the fields. I sit here alone, an old Faust separated from the world's joy by the wall of my abominable old age. They've no idea what old age means. During luncheon, they were all ears for what I was saying about business and the stock market. I was talking deliberately at Hubert, so that he might get out while there is still time. How worried he looked. . . . Not a born bluffer, our Hubert! He polished off his food. You had piled his plate with the obstinacy of an unhappy mother who sees that her son is devoured by anxiety and forces him to eat, as though that were so much to the good, were something gained. And his only thanks was to snap your head off. It was me and Mamma over again.

How careful young Phili was to keep my glass filled! What a show of interest his wife, Janine, exhibited in my well-being! "Grandpapa, you *oughtn't* to smoke, really you oughtn't: even one cigarette's too much. Are you *sure* they haven't made a mistake? Is this coffee really free of caffeine?" She's a poor hand at deception, poor dear: her voice gives her away. She's just like you in the early days of our marriage, when you used to put on an act. But that all went by the board when your first child was born, and you became yourself again. Until the day of her death, Janine will be a woman "in the know," repeating everything she hears, provided she thinks it gives her an air of distinction, trotting out second-hand views about this, that, and the other, and not understanding a word. How Phili, who's nothing if not natural, an unashamed scavenger, can bear to live with such a little half-wit, beats me. But, no, I'm wrong: one thing about her is perfectly genuine, and that's her passion for him. The reason she's so transparent is that nothing matters for her, nothing really exists for her, but her love.

After luncheon we all sat out on the steps. Janine and Phili kept their eyes fixed on Geneviève, like a couple of dogs begging for crumbs, while she looked at no one but you. You said "no" with an almost imperceptible shake of the head, at which Geneviève got up and turned to me:

"How about taking a turn with me, Papa?" You're all so frightened of me! I took pity on her. I had made up my mind not to budge, but, all the same, I got up and took her arm. We walked round the meadow. The family watched us from the steps.

She lost no time in coming to the point. "I wanted to have a word with you about Phili."

She was trembling. It's horrible to know that one's children are frightened of one. But at sixty-eight a man's not free to decide whether he shall seem unapproachable or not. By that age the general cast of our features is set, and the heart, when it finds that it can no longer give expression to its feelings, grows discouraged. . . . Geneviève had decided what she wanted to say, and out it all came in a rush. . . . It had to do, as I had expected, with Phili's buying a share in a broker's firm. She stressed the one point of all others best calculated to antagonize me—the fact that Phili's having nothing to do was a constant threat to Janine's married happiness. He was beginning to stray from the domestic hearth. I told her that a share in a broker's firm would merely serve to supply a man like her son-in-law with convenient alibis. She stood up for him. Phili was universally popular. Why should I be harder on him than Janine was? . . . I protested that I neither judged nor condemned him, that I took not the slightest interest in his love life.

"Why should I bother about him? He certainly doesn't bother about me."

"He admires you enormously."

This impudent lie gave me the chance to trot out what I was keeping up my sleeve.

"That's as may be, my dear, but it doesn't prevent your precious Phili from referring to me as the 'old crocodile.' It's no good denying it. Many's the time I've heard him say it behind my back . . . and I've no wish to deny the imputation: crocodile I am, and crocodile I shall remain. There's nothing to hope for from an old crocodile—except his death. And even when he's dead"—I was foolish enough to add—"even when he's dead, he can still be up to his old tricks." (I'm sorry I said that: it only roused her suspicions.)

She was knocked of a heap. She tried to explain it all away (as though I care two hoots what Phili calls me!). What I detest about him is his youth. How can she have the faintest idea what a hated and despised old man feels at the sight of a young creature in the pride of life, who has had showered upon him, from youth up, those very things that I have tasted only once in half a century? I loathe and detest all young men, and Phili more than most. Like a cat slipping silently through the window, he has padded into my house, attracted by the smell of what was inside. My granddaughter may not have had much in the way of a dowry—but, oh! her "expectations"—only over our dead bodies do young gentlemen get within touching distance of our children's "expectations"!

Then as Geneviève started snuffling and dabbing at her eyes, I adopted a tone of sweet reasonableness.

"After all, my dear, you've got a perfectly good husband in the rum trade. Surely dear Alfred can find some sort of a job for his son-in-law? Why should I be more generous than you are yourselves?"

Then she started to talk about poor Alfred. What a change! What contempt! What disgust! According to her, he's a mean-spirited coward who is drawing in his horns more every day. Once upon a time his business was a large and prosperous affair, but now there isn't a living in it for more than one person.

I congratulated her on having such a husband. When a storm's brewing one's got to shorten sail. The future, I said, belongs to men like Alfred who can take a limited view. In these days, the only hope of making a success of business is to keep going in a small way. She thought I was laughing at her. But I was voicing my profound belief—as is shown by the fact that I keep my own money under lock and key and won't even take chances with the savings bank.

We walked back to the house. Geneviève didn't dare to say another word. I was no longer leaning on her arm. The members of the family, seated in a circle, watched us coming and, no doubt, were already busy interpreting the unfavorable omens. It was obvious that our return had interrupted an argument between Hubert's little lot and Geneviève's. What an unholy squabble there would be over my pile if ever I agreed to relax my grip! Phili was the only one on his feet. The wind was blowing in his rebellious hair. He was wearing an open-necked shirt with short sleeves. I have a horror of these modern young men who look like athletic girls! His baby cheeks flushed scarlet when, in reply to Janine's stupid question—"Well, have you had a nice chat?"—I replied, very quietly, "We have been talking about an old crocodile. . . ."

Let me repeat, it's not because of that piece of ill-conditioned rudeness that I hate him. They've no idea what old age means. You can't imagine the torment of having had nothing out of life, of having nothing to look forward to but death, of feeling that there is no other world beyond this one, that the puzzle will never be explained, the key never given to us. . . . You haven't suffered what I have suffered. You never will suffer what I am suffering now. It is not for your death that the children are impatient. They are fond of you in their own way, they love you. . . . From the very first they took sides with you against me. I had a very warm feeling for them. I can remember Geneviève—this fat, forty-year-old woman who, a moment or two back, was trying to wheedle four hundred thousand-franc notes out of me for her scamp of a son-in-law, as a little girl perched on my knee. As soon as you saw me paying any attention to her, you called her away. . . . But if I go on mixing present and past like this, I shall never get to the end of my confession. I really must try to put a little order into my thoughts. . . .

VI

I don't think that I began to hate you from the first year after that disastrous night. My hatred grew, by slow degrees, as I came to realize how completely indifferent you were to me, how nothing really existed for you outside the circle of your pulling, screaming, greedy little scraps of humanity. You did not even notice how, though I was not yet thirty, I had become an overworked chancery barrister with a big reputation at the most important bar in all France after that of Paris. It was the Villenave case (1893) that gave me the chance to prove myself a great criminal lawyer as well (it is exceedingly rare to excel in both branches). You were the only person who remained deaf to the universal applause of my gifts as a pleader. That was the year, too, in which our misunderstandings turned to open warfare.

The notorious Villenave case set the seal on my reputation. It also gave a further twist to the vice that was crushing out my life. Perhaps up till then I had still retained a tiny shred of hope, but I saw now, beyond all power to doubt, that, so far as you were concerned, I had ceased to exist.

I wonder whether you remember the story of that Villenave couple? They had been married for twenty years and were still so devoted to one another that they had become almost a legend. People talked of being as "loving as the Villenaves." They lived with an only son of fifteen in their château at Ornon, just outside the city, seeing very few people, and utterly self-sufficient. "It's the sort of thing one reads about in books," said your mother, using one of those ready-made phrases the secret of which her granddaughter Geneviève has inherited. I don't mind betting that you have forgotten everything to do with their story. If I tell it over again now, you'll just laugh at me as you always did when I described my triumphs of cross-examination at the dinner table. . . . Well, that can't be helped.

One morning, their servant, who was doing the downstairs rooms, heard a pistol shot on the first floor, followed by a cry of pain. He rushed upstairs. The door of his master's bedroom was locked. He could hear low voices, the sound of things being moved about, and agitated steps in the bathroom. He kept on rattling the handle, and, in a moment or two, the door was opened. Villenave was lying on the bed in his nightshirt, covered in blood. Madame de Villenave, her hair disordered, and wearing a dressing gown, was standing at the foot of the bed with a revolver in her hand. She said: "I have wounded Monsieur de Villenave. Get a doctor, a surgeon, and the police inspector—hurry! I will stay here." They could get nothing more out of her than that single statement—"I have wounded my husband"—and this was confirmed by Monsieur de Villenave as soon as he was able to speak. He refused to give any further information.

The accused would do nothing about appointing counsel to represent her at the trial. I was entrusted—as the son-in-law of a friend of theirs—with her defense. She maintained an attitude of unshakable obstinacy. Though I went every day to see her in prison, I could get nothing out of her. The city was filled with the most ridiculous rumors. Personally, I was convinced of her innocence from the very first. She was accusing herself, and the husband who loved her remained completely acquiescent. What an unerring nose do the unloved have for the scent of passion in others! This woman was entirely possessed by conjugal love. She had not fired at her husband. Might it be that she had tried to fling herself between him and a rejected lover? There had been no visitor to the house since the previous evening . . . there was no intimate friend who came regularly to see them . . . well, it's all ancient history now, and I won't go into details.

Up to the morning of the day of the trial I had decided to adopt a purely negative attitude, and merely to argue that Madame de Villenave could not have committed the crime that she was as good as confessing. But, at the very last moment, the evidence of her son, Yves, or, rather (for in itself that evidence was quite unimportant and shed no light on the mystery), the beseeching and commanding look that his mother kept steadily fixed on him all the time he was in the witness box, as well as the obvious relief that she showed when he left it, told me the truth. I denounced the son. I described him as a morbid adolescent who had been driven to a jealous frenzy by the love lavished upon his father. I flung myself with a sort of passionate logic into a spur-of-the-moment argument that has since become famous, and in which Professor F——, on his own admission, found the essential germ of his theory. It has shed new light not only on the psychology of adolescence, but on the treatment of its neuroses.

If I stir these old memories, it is not, my dear Isa, because I have the slightest hope of rousing in you, after forty years, the admiration that you did not feel at the moment of my triumph when my picture was appearing in the newspapers of two hemispheres. Your complete indifference in this supremely important moment of my career revealed to me the extent of my solitude and abandonment. But there was more to it than that. For weeks on end I had had before my eyes, between the four walls of a cell, a woman who was sacrificing herself with the sole purpose of saving, not so much *her* child, as her husband's, the heir to his name. It was he, the victim, who had implored her to take the blame. So great was her love that she had been willing to let the world believe that she was a criminal, that she had tried to murder the man whom she adored to the exclusion of everybody and everything in the world. Conjugal, not maternal, love had been the mainspring of her action (as was proved by the sequel, for she separated from her son and has always found some excuse or other for living away from him ever since). I, too, might have been loved as Villenave was loved. Of him, too, I saw a good deal at the time of the trial. What had he got that I hadn't? True, he was well-born and averagely good-looking, but I don't think he was very intelligent. His hostile attitude to me after the trial proved that. I, on the other hand, was in my own way something of a genius. If, at that moment, I had been blessed with a wife who loved me, to what heights might I not have risen? Nobody can go on indefinitely believing in himself unless he gets some help from outside. There must be some other person to give him assurance of his abilities, someone to crown him when the day of recognition comes. When, as a schoolboy, I used to walk back from the dais on prize day, with my arms full of books, it was always my mother's eyes that I tried to catch in the crowd, and it was she who, to the sound of a military band, really placed the laurel wreath upon my freshly cropped head.

At the time of the Villenave case she was beginning to fail, though I realized it only by degrees. The extent to which she was entirely wrapped up in a little black dog, which barked furiously every time I approached her, gave me my first inkling of her declining powers. Whenever I went to see her, she would talk about nothing else. She no longer listened to anything I said.

In any case, her feeling for me could never have been a substitute for the love that might have saved me at this turning point of my life. Her ruling vice was the love of money, and this I have inherited. The passion is in my blood. She would have done everything she could to keep me in a profession that, to use her own words, brought in "big money." At that time, the idea of writing attracted me. Many newspapers, and all the important reviews, approached me with offers. In addition, the Left-wing parties wanted me to stand at the next election for the constituency of La Bastide (the man who finally accepted, in my place, got in without the slightest difficulty), but I refused to listen to the call of my ambitions because I didn't want to give up the chance of earning "big money."

In that, I was falling in with your wishes, too. You had made it quite clear to me that you would never leave the provinces. A genuinely loving wife would have taken pleasure in my fame, would have taught me that the art of living consists in abandoning a base passion for one more noble. Those idiot journalists who make a great show of indignation when some man of law takes advantage of his position as a deputy or a minister to enjoy a few trivial pickings would be better employed in expressing admiration of those who have succeeded in establishing an intelligent hierarchy among their passions and have preferred glory in the field of politics to big profits in business. If you had had any real love for me you could have saved me from my ingrained habit of never setting anything above immediate gain, of being incapable of giving up the mediocre and squalid temptation of big fees for the shadow of power. After all, there is no shadow without a reality that projects it. The very shadow itself is a reality. As things turned out, there was nothing for me to do but go on making "big money," just like the grocer at the corner.

That's all I have left—the money I earned in the course of those terrible years, the money you're mad enough to want me to give away. The very idea that you might enjoy it after my death is intolerable to me. I told you at the beginning of this screed that I had, at one time, taken steps to see that you should be left with nothing, at the same time giving you reason to believe that I had now abandoned this particular plan of revenge. But I had not then taken into account the tidal movement of my hatred. Sometimes it ebbs, and I grow soft . . . sometimes it flows, and then the muddy waters engulf me.

After what happened today, after this Easter incident, this concerted attack undertaken with the object of stripping me bare in the interests of dear Phili, I feel differently. I have had a view of the family pack sitting back on its hunkers round the door and spying on my movements. I am obsessed by the idea of so dividing up my property that you'll all be at one another's throats. Oh yes, you'll fight like dogs over the land and over the securities. Don't bother—you're going to get the land all right, but the securities no longer exist. The ones I mentioned on the first page of this letter I sold last week at the top of the market. Since then, they've been falling every day. Ships have a way of foundering as soon as I abandon them. I'm never wrong. My millions of liquid capital you shall have—but only if I decide in your favor. There are days when I make up my mind not to leave you a penny of it.

I can hear the whole lot of you whispering your way upstairs. You stop: you talk freely without fear of waking me (the accepted view is that I am deaf). I can see the light of your candles underneath the door. I recognize Phili's falsetto (anybody would think his voice is still breaking) and catch a sudden burst of stifled laughter, the sound of young women clucking. You're calling them to order: you're just going to say—"He isn't asleep, I know he isn't." . . . You creep up to my door; you listen; you look through the keyhole. The lamp gives me away. You've returned to the pack. I think you must be whispering—"He's still awake; he's listening to you. . . ."

They tiptoe away; the stairs creak; door after door closes. On this Easter night the house is full of couples. I might be the living trunk from which these young shoots have sprung. Most fathers are beloved: but you were my enemy, and my children have gone over to the enemy.

It is to this war between us that I must turn now. I feel too weak to go on writing, yet hate the thought of going to bed, even of lying down in the rare moments when the state of my heart permits it. At my age, sleep attracts the attention to death. One mustn't look as though one were dead. I have a feeling that so long as I am on my feet death can't come near me. What is it that I dread about death?—physical pain? the awful struggle at the end?—no, not that, but the feeling that to die is to become nothing, that our state in the grave can be expressed only by the symbol ———.

VII

So long as our three little ones remained in the limbo of infancy, the enmity between us was still disguised. But there was a heavy atmosphere about our home. Your indifference to me, your complete detachment from everything that had to do with me, kept you from feeling any discomfort on that account, or even from noticing it. Besides, I was never there. I lunched alone at eleven, so as to get to the courts by midday. Work took up most of my time and—well, you can guess what I did with such brief snatches of leisure as I might have been able to give my family. Why did I turn to this hideous, bare skeleton of debauchery? It was stripped of everything that usually provides some excuse even for animal passion. It had been reduced to pure horror, without a hint of feeling to justify it, without the least pretense of sentiment. I might so easily have had the kind of adventures that the world approves. A lawyer of my age could scarcely avoid certain temptations. There were many young women ready and eager to get under the skin of the public figure and rouse the man. . . . But I had lost faith in the creatures, or, rather, in my power to attract any of them. I at once detected the self-interest that animated those who were "ready and willing," those of whose charms I was conscious. The fixed idea that what they were looking for was a certain security of tenure chilled my ardor. Why should I mind admitting that, in addition to the tragic certainty of feeling myself to be somebody whom no one would ever love, I was a victim to the suspicion that afflicts most rich men and makes them feel that they are being deceived and exploited? I had put you on a fixed allowance, and you knew me too well to expect a penny more than the agreed sum. It was calculated on a generous basis, and you never exceeded it. I felt no threat of danger from that quarter. But with other women it was quite a different kettle of fish! I was one of those fools who believe that there are only two classes of women—those who indulge in love for its own sake, and those debased creatures who are out only for what they can get. In fact, most women oscillate between the two. They want to give free rein to their amorous tendencies, and they want to be "kept," protected and spoiled. At sixty-eight I look back with a lucidity, which, at times, makes me want to howl, at all that I rejected in those days, not from any sense of virtue, but because I was mistrustful and cowardly. The few "affairs" that I did begin soon ended, either because my naturally suspicious nature misinterpreted even the most innocent of requests, or because I made myself odious by reason of those manias of mine that you know only too well—endless quarrels with waiters or cab drivers on the subject of tips. I like to know in advance precisely what I've got to pay. I like to work to a tariff. It's not easy to confess this. What I found attractive in mercenary love was, probably, that it had a fixed price. But in a man of my sort what possible connection could there be between mere self-indulgence and the cravings of the heart? I had ceased to believe that the cravings of the heart could ever be satisfied, and I took good care to stifle them as soon as they showed their heads. I was a past master in the art of destroying all sentiment at the precise moment when the will begins to play a decisive part in matters of love, when a man can still stand on the sidelines of passion and is free to surrender or to hold back while there is still time. I chose the simplest satisfactions—those that may be had for an agreed outlay. I hate being "done," but what I owe I pay. You're always girding at me for being "close," but that doesn't prevent me from having a horror of debts. I pay cash for everything. My tradesmen know this and bless me. I can't bear the thought that I owe any man a penny. Love, I thought, was something in which one was perpetually giving . . . and I found it disgusting.

Perhaps I'm making too much of all this and fouling my own nest. I have loved, and even perhaps been loved. It was in 1909, when my youth was already on the wane. Why should I pass over that particular adventure in silence? You knew all about it. You made no bones about recalling it when you wanted to drive me into a corner.

She was a young schoolteacher who had been charged with infanticide, and I saved her. She gave herself to me at first out of sheer gratitude, but later . . . yes, for one year I knew what real love was. What ruined everything was my inability to keep my demands in check. Not content with letting her live in mean circumstances, which were only just one degree above actual poverty, I had to have her constantly at my beck and call. I never let her see anybody. She always had to be there when I wanted her during my brief periods of leisure, and not there when I didn't. She was my property. My passion for possession, and for using and abusing what I possess, extends to human beings. I ought to have been a slave owner. For this one and only time I thought I had found a victim really made to the measure of my demands. I kept a close watch even on the expression of her face. . . . But I'm forgetting my promise not to tell you about this side of my life. The long and the short of it is that she ran away to Paris. She couldn't stand it any longer.

"It's not only us you can't get on with. Everyone's afraid of you and keeps out of your way. You must know that, Louis!" If you've said that once, you've said it a hundred times, and it's perfectly true. At the law courts I was always a lone wolf. I was elected to the bar council—but only at the last possible moment. They'd chosen too many fools in my stead for me ever to be ambitious of the presidency. I'm not sure, as a matter of fact, that I ever really wanted it. It would have meant being a representative, entertaining. Honors like that cost a deal of money, and the game's not worth the candle. You wanted it for the sake of the children. You've never wanted anything for me. "Do it for the sake of the children."

During the year immediately following our marriage, your father had his first stroke, and the château of Cenon was closed to us. You very quickly adopted Calèse. The only thing of mine you've ever really made your own is my land. You took root in my soil, but our roots never met. Your children spent all their holidays in this house and garden. Our little Marie died here. But, so far from her death giving you a horror of the place, you have invested the room in which she lived her last days with a sort of sacred character. . . . It was here that you hatched your brood, that you tended the sick, watched by the cradles, and sent an endless succession of nurses and governesses packing. It was on lines strung to the apple trees that Marie's tiny dresses were hung out to dry, and a long sequence of innocent garments. It was in this drawing room that the Abbé Ardouin used to group the children round the piano and make them sing choruses that, so as to avoid my anger, were not always sacred in character.

Smoking in front of the house on summer evenings, I used to hear their pure young voices. I can still recollect that air of Lulli's, *"Ah! que ces bois, ces rochers, ces fontaines. . . ."* There was about it all a sense of quiet happiness from which I felt myself excluded. It was a zone of dreamlike innocence that I was forbidden to enter. It was a quiet sea of love that died into nothingness a few feet from the rock of my presence.

When I entered the drawing room, the voices fell silent. Geneviève took herself off with a book. Marie was the only one who wasn't frightened of me. I called to her, and she came. I snatched her up in my arms, and she nestled there happily enough. I could feel her little bird's heart beating. I let her go, and at once she fluttered away into the garden. . . . Marie!

Very early on the children began to show surprise at my absence from Mass, and at my Friday cutlet. But the struggle that you and I were waging very rarely flared up when they were present, and if it did, I was usually beaten. After each one of my defeats, the war went underground again. Calèse was the battlefield, for when we were in Bordeaux, I was scarcely ever at home. But the legal vacation coincided with the school holidays, and August and September found us all together here.

I remember one occasion when we had a head-on clash (it had to do with some joke I had made in Geneviève's hearing, when she was reciting her Scripture lesson). I asserted my right to defend my children's minds; you, yours to protect their souls.

I had been routed once already when I agreed that Hubert should be entrusted to the Jesuit Fathers and the younger children to the Ladies of the Sacred Heart. I had yielded to the prestige that the traditions of the Fondaudège family always enjoyed in my eyes. But I was hungry for revenge, and, on that particular occasion, what mattered to me was that I had hit on the one subject capable of making you really wild. When *that* was under discussion, you had to abandon your attitude of indifference and listen to what I was saying, no matter how much you might hate it. At last I had found a way of bringing you to battle. Formerly my irreligion had been no more than a mold into which I ran the various humiliations that, as the son of a peasant father who had made money, I had had to endure from my superior middle-class companions. But now I filled it with all the frustrations I had met with in love, and an almost limitless extent of rancorous resentment.

The dispute started again during luncheon (I had asked what possible satisfaction it could give the Eternal Being to see you eating salmon trout instead of boiled beef). You left the table. I remember the expression on the children's faces, I followed you to your room. Your eyes were dry: you spoke quite calmly. I realized then that you hadn't been so wholly unaware of the life I had been leading as I had supposed. You had come across certain letters that contained quite enough evidence to get you a separation. "I have stayed with you for the sake of the children," you said. "But if your presence here is going to endanger their spiritual well-being, I shall not hesitate for a moment."

No, you certainly would not have hesitated to leave both me and my money. Ruled though you might be by self-interest, you would have consented to any sacrifice that might have been necessary to keep the teachings of the church—that agglomeration of habits, formulae, and general nonsense—unsullied in those little brains.

I did not keep the letter of abuse you sent me after Marie's death. You were too strong for me. Any legal proceedings between us would seriously have imperiled my own position. In those days, and in provincial circles, such things were not taken lightly. There was already a rumor going about to the effect that I was a Freemason. My opinions had made me more or less of an outcast from local society. But for the prestige enjoyed by your family, they might have done me a lot of harm. Worst of all, had there been a legal separation, I should have had to surrender the Suez Canal shares that formed part of your dowry. I had come to regard them as my own property. I couldn't face the thought of having to give them up—(to say nothing of the allowance your father made us).

I ate humble pie and agreed to all the conditions you laid down. But I made up my mind to devote my leisure to the task of winning over the children. I came to that decision at the beginning of August 1896. Those sad and blazing summers of long ago have become confused in my mind, and my memories of that time cover a period of, roughly, five years (1895–1900).

I thought it would not be difficult to renew my hold over the children. I reckoned on my authority as their father and on my intelligence. It would be a mere nothing, I thought, to work on a boy of ten and two little girls. I remember the surprise and uneasiness that they showed when I suggested one day that they should go for a long walk with Papa. You were sitting in the courtyard, under the silver lime. They looked at you inquiringly. "There's no need for you to ask my permission, my pets!"

We started off. How does one talk to children? Accustomed though I am to standing up to the public prosecutor, to defending counsel when I'm appearing for the defendant in a civil suit, to a whole courtful of hostile lawyers, and though assize judges go in fear of me, I confess that children get me down—children and members of the lower orders, even peasants, though I am a peasant's son myself. In their presence I become unsure of myself and tongue-tied.

They were very nice to me, but obviously on their guard. You had long ago thrown a holding force into those three hearts! You controlled all the approaches. Not one step could I take without your permission. You had made no attempt to undermine my authority—oh, you were far too scrupulous for that! but you had let them see pretty clearly that a lot of praying would have to be done for poor Papa. No matter how erring I might be, I occupied a perfectly definite place in their scheme of things—I was the "poor Papa," the object of their prayers, the misguided pagan ripe for conversion—and anything I might say or hint on the subject of religion merely confirmed the rather crude idea they had of me.

They lived in a world of marvels. Its landmarks were the feast days of the year, each of them celebrated with solemn piety. *You* could get them to do anything you wanted just by talking about the first communion that they had either made recently or were about to make. When, in the evening, they sang on the front steps at Calèse, it was not always the airs of Lulli—which were included for my especial delectation: there were psalms, too. From far away I could see the vague blur made by your little group, and, when there was a moon, could make out the three little lifted faces. The sound of my footsteps on the gravel interrupted their singing.

On Sundays I was awakened by the bustle you all made in getting off to Mass. You were always afraid of being late. The horses pawed the ground; the cook hadn't turned up and had to be called. One of the children had forgotten a prayer book. A shrill voice cried: "Which Sunday after Pentecost is it?"

When they got back and came in to give me a kiss they always found me still in bed. Little Marie, who must have recited all the prayers she knew with a special "intention" for me, stared solemnly into my face, doubtless hoping to discover some slight improvement in my spiritual state.

She was the only one of them who did not irritate me. The two elder were already smugly ensconced in the beliefs to which you clung with so sure a feeling for that middle-class comfort that, at a later date, was to make them turn their backs on all the heroic virtues and sublime lunacies of the Christian faith. In her, on the contrary, there was a touching ardor, a genuine feeling of compassion for the farm laborers and the poor. People said of her: "She'd give everything she has: money just trickles through her fingers. It's all very charming, of course, but that sort of generosity needs careful watching. . . ." They said, too: "No one can resist her, not even her father." She used to climb on my knee of an evening of her own accord. Once she fell asleep with her head on my shoulder. Her curls tickled my cheek. I was suffering agonies because I had to keep so still and I wanted to smoke. But I sat there like a graven image, and, when the nurse came to fetch her at nine o'clock, I carried her all the way up to her room. You all stared at me in amazement, as though I had been the wild beast in the legend who licked the feet of the child martyrs. Shortly after that—it was on the morning of the fourteenth of August, she said to me—you know how children do:

"Promise—there's something I want to ask you, but you must promise first to do what I say. . . ."

She reminded me that you were going to sing at the eleven o'clock Mass next day and that it would be nice of me to go and listen.

"You've promised! You've promised!" she kept on saying as she kissed me: "you've given your word!"

She took my kiss for a promise. The whole house was told about it. I felt that I was under observation. The "master" was going to Mass next day—fancy that! he who never, as a rule, put his foot inside a church! It was an event of immense significance.

I sat down to dinner that evening in a mood of irritability that I could not long conceal. Hubert asked you something—I forget what—about Dreyfus. I remember protesting furiously against your reply and leaving the room. I did not come back, but packed my bag, took the 6 AM train on the fifteenth, and spent a hideous day in Bordeaux where the heat was stifling and everybody seemed to have gone away.

It seems odd to me now that you should ever have seen me again at Calèse after that. How came it that I always spent the school holidays with the family instead of in traveling? No doubt I could concoct all sorts of admirable explanations, but the real truth was my dislike of incurring a double expense. The idea that anyone could set off on a trip and spend a lot of money without first emptying the larder and locking up the house never occurred to me. All the pleasure of going away would have been ruined for me by the knowledge that the household expenses were piling up all the time. So, I just crawled back to the family swill pail. There was food waiting for me at Calèse, so why should I feed elsewhere? My mother had bequeathed to me her mania for "economy," and I had made a virtue of it.

Back I came, then, but with such resentment in my heart that not even Marie could soften me. I began to use tactics of a different kind against you. Instead of delivering a frontal attack on your beliefs, I did all I could, no matter how trivial the circumstances, to show how ill your practice squared with your faith. You must admit, my poor Isa, that, good Christian though you were, I had an easy enough task! You had forgotten, if, indeed, you had ever known, that charity is synonymous with love. You gave its name to what you regarded as your duties to the poor. These you scrupulously observed, always with a weather eye open on your eternal salvation! I realize that a profound change has come over you in recent years. Today you visit cancer cases in hospital—I know all about that: but, at the time I am speaking of, once you had helped the poor—

your poor—you felt all the freer to demand from those who were dependent on you what you regarded as your due. You made no compromise with the duty of the housewife, which is to get the largest possible amount of work in return for the lowest possible wages. The wretched old crone who came every morning to our front door with her cart could never sell you so much as a lettuce without your whittling down her meager profit to the last farthing. If she had been a beggar, you would have given freely of your "charity."

When your frightened servants ventured to ask you for a "rise," you were at first amazed and then so furiously indignant that you always ended by getting your way. You had a sort of genius for being able to demonstrate that they really had all they could reasonably want. You managed to pile up the total of their advantages: "You have a roof over your heads, a cask of wine, and half of a pig that you fatten on my potatoes, to say nothing of a garden in which you can grow vegetables." The poor devils never realized, till you told them, how well off they were! Your maid, you said, could save every penny of the forty francs you paid her every month! "She gets all my old clothes and underlinen and shoes. What can she find to spend her money *on?* If I gave her more, she'd only hand it over to her family!"

I admit, of course, that you looked after them devotedly when they were ill. You never left them to their own resources. I am well aware that you were, for the most part, always respected, and sometimes loved, by your staff. It is the foible of domestics to despise weak mistresses. In all such matters you were a true representative of the ideas of your class and period. But you could never bring yourself to admit that the Gospel condemned them. "*I* always thought"—I would say—"that Christ laid it down . . ." Remarks of that kind invariably brought you up short. You didn't know what to answer, and you were furious because of the children. You unfailingly finished up by falling into the trap. "We're not meant to take those things literally . . ." you would stammer, and that gave me just the chance I needed to triumph over you. I would floor you with examples, all going to show that sanctity consists, precisely, in taking the Gospels literally. If you were foolish enough to reply that you were not a saint, I would quote the precept: "Be ye perfect, even as your Father in heaven is perfect."

You must admit, my poor Isa, that I did what I could in my own way, and that if, now, you visit cancer cases, it is to me in part that they owe your devotion! In the old days, your love of your children obsessed you to the exclusion of every other consideration. All your reserves of kindness and self-sacrifice were used up on them. They filled your vision: you couldn't *see* anybody else. It wasn't only from me that they had alienated you, but from the whole of the rest of the world. The only thing you could speak about to God was their health and their future. That's where I got my chance. I would ask whether, as a Christian, you ought not rather to demand for them every kind of cross—poverty, sickness. You would cut me short: "I'm not going to answer you: you're talking about what you don't understand. . . ." Unfortunately for you, we had as a tutor a young seminarist of twenty-three, the Abbé Ardouin. I was merciless in my appeals to him for support and caused him much embarrassment, since I never asked his opinion except when I knew that I was in the right. He was incapable of saying anything but what he really thought. As the Dreyfus case developed, I found innumerable opportunities for setting him at odds with you. "So you're in favor"—you would say—"of undermining our whole military system for a . . ." The mere word "Jew" released the full spate of my pretended indignation, and I would keep on until I had forced the abbé to admit that no true Christian ought to connive at the condemnation of an innocent man, even though the safety of the country might be at stake.

But I made no attempt to convince you and the children, whose whole knowledge of the "affair" was derived from caricatures that appeared in the "right-thinking" newspapers. You closed your ranks against me and presented an impenetrable front. Even when I seemed to be in the right, you suspected me of trickery. Things got to such a pitch that you deliberately said nothing when I was within earshot. I had only to come near—and it's just the same now—for all discussion to stop. But there were times when I hid in the shrubbery without your knowing I was there, and then I would put in my oar before you had time to retreat. You couldn't avoid the issue then.

Talking of the Abbé Ardouin to your friends, you would say: "The man's a perfect saint. He's no more capable of thinking evil than a child. My husband plays with him like a cat with a mouse. That's the only reason he puts up with him. As a rule, he hates the very sight of a cassock. . . ."

The only reason I'd agreed to having a priest for tutor was, as a matter of fact, that no layman would have agreed to work all through the holidays for 150 francs. At first I treated the tall, black-haired, shy young man with the weak eyes as completely insignificant. I took no more notice of him than I did of the furniture. He saw to it that the children did their work, took them out for walks, ate very little, and never uttered a word. As soon as dinner was finished, he went up to his room. Sometimes, when there was nobody about, he played the piano. I know nothing of music, but he was, as you said, "a nice person to have about the place."

One incident there was that I am sure you have not forgotten. What you have never known is that it established between the Abbé Ardouin and me a secret current of sympathy. One day the children told me that the curé had called. I at once took refuge in the vineyard, as I always did on such occasions.

But you sent Hubert to fetch me back. The curé had something urgent to say to me. With much grumbling I returned to the house, because I was really rather frightened of the little old man. He had come, he said, to unburden his conscience. It was he who had recommended the Abbé Ardouin as a thoroughly reliable young seminarist who had been prevented, by ill health, from taking orders at the normal time. He had just learned, in the course of a retreat, that this postponement had actually been a disciplinary measure. The abbé was, to be sure, very pious, but he was mad about music and had been tempted by one of his coseminarists to slip out one night and go to a charity concert at the Grand Theatre. They were in lay dress but were recognized and denounced. What made matters worse was that one of the performers was Madame Georgette Lebrun, and she had sung excerpts from *Thaïs*. At sight of her bare feet and Greek tunic, held up under the arms by a silver girdle ("and that was all: not so much as a hint of a shoulder strap"), there had been an "Oh!" of indignation. In the Union Club Box an old gentleman had exclaimed: "This is really going a bit *too* far . . . where does she think she is?" Such was the spectacle to which the Abbé Ardouin had been exposed. One of the delinquents had suffered immediate expulsion: the other—the abbé—had been pardoned. He was a prize student. But his superiors had postponed his ordination for two years.

We were all of us unanimous in declaring that he enjoyed our full confidence. From then on, however, the curé showed the greatest coldness to the young man who, he said, had deceived him. No doubt you remember the incident. What you have never known is that, on the same evening, while I was smoking on the terrace, I saw coming toward me in the moonlight the emaciated figure of the guilty man. He addressed me with considerable embarrassment and asked to be forgiven for having introduced himself into my family without first explaining that there was a slur upon his character. When I told him that the escapade that had caused all the trouble made me like him the more, he suddenly adopted an intransigent attitude and proceeded to argue against himself. I couldn't, he said, realize the heinousness of his offense. It was not merely that he had broken his vow of obedience: he had sinned against his vocation and against the moral code. He had been a cause of scandal. The whole of the rest of his life would not be long enough to enable him to make proper reparation for his misdeed. . . . I can still see that tall, bowed back, and his shadow in the moonlight, cut in two by the parapet of the terrace.

Prejudiced though I might be against men of his cloth, I could not, witnessing his shame and sorrow, suspect him of the faintest tinge of hypocrisy. He excused his silence to us on the ground of his need. But for the job we had offered him, he would have had to live for two months at the cost of his mother, a poor widow of Libourne, who went out charring. When I replied that, so far as I could see, there had been no obligation upon him to mention something that had to do merely with seminary discipline, he took my hand and uttered the following extraordinary words. It was the first time that anything of the sort had been said to me, and I don't mind confessing that I felt knocked sideways.

"You are," he said, "a very good man." You know that laugh of mine that, even in our first years together, got on your nerves, that sort of private chortle that has the effect of killing any gaiety within the radius of my presence?—well, it racked me that evening as I looked at the shocked and gawky seminarist in front of me. After a while I was able to get out:

"You can't know, Monsieur l'Abbé, how comic that sounds. Ask those who know me whether I am good! Question my family, my professional colleagues! Why, malevolence is my leading characteristic!"

He replied, rather shyly, that those who are truly malevolent don't talk about it.

"I defy you," said I, "to find what you would call a single good action in the whole course of my life."

Then, intending a reference to my calling, he quoted the words of Christ: "I was in prison, and ye visited Me. . . ."

"That's how I make my living, Monsieur l'Abbé. I act from purely self-interested motives. There was a time when I even bribed the jailers to mention my name, at suitable moments, to those awaiting trial . . . not much goodness there, eh?"

I have forgotten what he said to that. We strolled together under the lime trees. How surprised you'd have been if I had told you that the presence of that frocked priest somehow brought me peace of mind. But it did.

It was my habit to get up before sunrise and go down into the garden to breathe the morning coolness. On those occasions I used to watch the abbé setting off for Mass. He walked quickly and was so much absorbed in his own thoughts that he sometimes passed quite close to me without so much as being aware of my presence. Those were the days when I was lashing you with my mockeries and doing everything I could to prove that your actions were at odds with your principles. . . . Nevertheless, my conscience was not altogether comfortable. Each time I caught you out in some meanness, some lack of charity, I pretended that there was not a trace of Christ's spirit among the lot of you. But I knew perfectly well, all the time, that beneath my roof, and unsuspected by the other inmates, there dwelt a man who lived in strict obedience to its promptings.

VIII

There was one occasion, however, when you really did fill me with genuine and unfeigned horror. At some time in '96 or '97—you will remember the exact date—our brother-in-law the Baron Philipot died. Your sister, Marinette, woke one morning and said something to him. He did not answer. She opened the shutters and saw the old man's upturned eyes and sagging jaw. It took her quite a little while to realize that she had been sleeping for a considerable time beside a corpse.

I don't think any of you fully realized the beastliness of that old wretch's will. He left his wife an enormous fortune, on one condition—that she should never marry again. If she did so, the bulk of the money was to go to his nephews.

"We shall have to take great care of her," your mother kept on saying. "Fortunately, we are a very united family. The poor darling mustn't be left alone for a moment."

At that time Marinette was about thirty, though she looked, as you will remember, little more than a girl. She had let herself be married off to an old man without a word of protest and had put up with him very patiently. It never occurred to you that she might find some difficulty in shouldering the responsibilities of perpetual widowhood. You entirely discounted the shock of her release, the effect upon her of emerging suddenly from a dark tunnel into the full light of day.

Don't be afraid, Isa, that I am going to abuse the advantage that the situation offered me. It was only natural that you should want all those millions to stay in the family, that you should hope our children would ultimately enjoy them. It was wrong, you thought, that Marinette should get no reward for ten years of slavery to an old man's whim. You behaved as all good parents would have behaved in the circumstances. Celibacy seemed to you to be a perfectly natural condition. I don't suppose you remembered the time when you had been a young wife. That chapter had been long since closed. You were a mother. The other implications of marriage had ceased to exist for you and for your parents. Imagination has never been an outstanding characteristic of your family. In this matter of sexual relationships, your attitude was neither that of brute beasts nor of ordinary human beings.

It was agreed that Marinette should spend the first summer of her widowhood at Calèse. She accepted the suggestion gladly, not that there was much intimacy between you, but she was fond of our children and especially of Marie. I scarcely knew her. What at first struck me about her was her

of her late husband. A woman always thinks of ideas, whether about religion or anything else in terms of a *person*. For her, they take tangible form, and the form may be either hated or adored. It would not have been difficult for me to take advantage of rebellious youth; but though I found it easy enough to act as her echo so long as it was all of *you* she inveighed against, I found it impossible to approve the contemptuous way in which she spoke of the millions she would lose in the event of her marrying again. I had every reason in the world to agree with her, and to take a high line of romantic nobility, but I could not pretend, even halfheartedly, to agree with her when she spoke of the loss of such a fortune as something not worth worrying about. If I am to be perfectly frank, I think I ought to admit that the idea of her dying, and of the money coming to us, was not wholly absent from my mind (and when I say "us," I don't mean the children—to whom I scarcely gave a thought—but, primarily, to myself).

Try as I might to school myself to use the words she would have liked to hear, it was no good. What I actually said was: "My dear Marinette, you can't be serious! Think of it, seven million! It is impossible to be indifferent to seven million! No man in the world is worth the sacrifice of even a fraction of such a sum!"—and, when she maintained that happiness was more important than money, I told her that nobody could give up such a fortune and be happy.

"It's all very well for you to say you hate them!" she exclaimed: "You're really one of them, you know!"

Then she set off at a gallop, with me following. Her verdict had been passed on me: all hope was lost. What a price I was paying for my lunatic love of money! I might have found in Marinette a younger sister, a mistress. . . . You'd like me, wouldn't you, to sacrifice to you that to which I've sacrificed everything else? Oh, no, my money's cost me far too dear for me to give up a single penny of it until I've breathed my last!

But you never give up, do you? I can't help wondering whether Hubert's wife, who forced her presence on me last Sunday, was really acting as your delegate or whether she came of her own accord. Poor Olympe! (why on earth did Phili nickname her Olympe?—we've all forgotten what her real name is) . . . on the whole, I'm inclined to believe that she said nothing to you about her coming to see me. You've never made her one of yourselves, you don't regard her as belonging to the family. She is completely indifferent to everything, outside the boundaries of her narrow world. She knows nothing of the laws of the "tribe" and has no idea that I am "the enemy." That's not because she is either benevolent or sympathetic, but simply because she never thinks about other people and doesn't even bother to hate them.

"He's always very nice to me," she says whenever my name is mentioned in her hearing. She is entirely unaware of my bitterness, and because, simply from a spirit of contradiction, I take up the cudgels in her favor against the lot of you, is convinced that I find her attractive.

Reading between the lines of her confused outpourings, I gather that Hubert has "got out" in time, but that he has had to call on the whole of his private fortune, as well as on his wife's dowry, to save the business. "He says he's bound to get his money back, but that he must have an advance . . . he calls it a mortgage on his expectations. . . ."

When she said that, I nodded my head. I agreed with everything and pretended not to have the remotest idea what it was she wanted. I can play the innocent very successfully at such times!

If only poor Olympe knew what I sacrificed to money in the days when I was still relatively young!

On those mornings of my thirty-fifth year, we used to jog back, your sister and I, letting the horses take their own pace, along the road, which was already feeling the heat of the sun, between the sprayed vines. She sat there in the saddle mocking at me while I talked about the millions that she mustn't, on any account, lose. Each time that I managed to free myself from the obsession of that menaced fortune, she would laugh at me with a sort of contemptuous kindness. I tried to defend myself, but only succeeded in getting into deeper water.

"It's in your own interest, Marinette, that I'm talking like this. You don't really think, do you, that I'm the sort of man to let himself be hagridden by the problem of his children's future? I know that Isa doesn't want the money to slip between their fingers, but I . . ."

Then she would laugh and say between partly clenched teeth:

"You're quite horrid enough as it is. . . ."

I protested that I was thinking only of her happiness. She shook her head with an air of disgust. What really made her envious, though she never admitted it, was not so much marriage as motherhood.

Oh, she despised me all right! But when, after luncheon, in spite of the heat, I left the dark, cool house where the members of the family were dozing, sprawled on the leather sofas and in the wicker chairs, when I threw back the shutters of the French windows and slipped out into the blazing blue, I didn't have to look back. I knew perfectly well that she would follow. I could hear her footsteps on the gravel. She walked with difficulty, catching her high heels in the baked earth. We stood together with our elbows on the parapet of the terrace. She played a sort of game with herself, which consisted in seeing how long she could keep her bare arm on the hot stone.

The plain beneath gave itself to the sun in a silence as deep as when it sleeps under the moon. The Landes ringed the horizon in an immense black semicircle on which the metallic sky pressed like a weight. Not a man, not an animal, would stir out of doors till four o'clock. The flies buzzed but made no effort to move away. They were no less motionless than the pillar of smoke rising from the plain straight and still in the airless heat.

I knew that the woman at my side could never love me, that everything about me was odious to her. But we were the only two living things in that lost land, imprisoned in its summer torpor. She was young and tormented, spied upon by her family, and she turned to me as unconsciously as the heliotrope turns to the sun. And yet, had I betrayed by a single word the emotions of my heart, she would have given me only mockery in return. I was perfectly well aware that she would have repulsed with disgust any advances on my part, however timid. There we stood together, on the edge of that immense vat in which the future harvest of the grapes was fermenting under the blue-tinted leaves, drowsing in the sun.

And what did you think, Isa, about those morning rides and close confabulations while the rest of the world was sunk in siesta? I know what you thought, because on one occasion I overheard you. Through the closed shutters of the drawing room I heard you say to your mother, who was staying with us at Calèse (no doubt she had come to reinforce the watch that was being kept on Marinette):

"He's a bad influence on her, but only because of his ideas. Apart from them he serves as a distraction. I can see no harm in their going about together."

"Yes, he *is* a distraction for her, and that's all that really matters," your mother replied.

You were delighted to think that I was a distraction for Marinette. "But after the holidays," you said more than once, "we shall have to find some other way of keeping her amused." You may have despised me, Isa, but your contempt was nothing to mine when I heard you talk like that. I suppose it never occurred to you that there might be any danger. Women have a way of not remembering what they have ceased to feel.

Nothing, to be sure, could possibly happen during those after-luncheon intimacies poised above the plain. Empty though the world was, we were standing, as it were, bang in the middle of a stage. Had there been but one peasant who had not surrendered to siesta, he would have been bound to see us there, a man and a woman motionless as two trees, gazing down at the incandescent earth, and so close together that neither could have made the slightest movement without touching the other.

But our nightly strolls were no less innocent. I remember one August evening in particular. Dinner had been made stormy by a discussion of the Dreyfus case. Marinette, who, with me, represented the party for revision, had by now surpassed me in the art of bringing the Abbé Ardouin into the open and forcing him into taking sides. You had mentioned with enthusiasm some article of Drumont's, and Marinette, as though butter wouldn't melt in her mouth, had said:

"Do tell me, Monsieur l'Abbé, is it permissible for us to hate the Jews?"

That evening, much to our delight, he did not take refuge in easy evasions. He spoke of the greatness of the chosen people, of the part they had played as witnesses to the truth, of their conversion, which had been foretold and would herald the end of the world. And when Hubert protested that we needs must hate our Lord's butchers, the Abbé replied that each of us had the right to hate one of Christ's butchers, and one only—himself, but no one else.

Thoroughly put out, you retorted that the only result of such highfalutin theories would be the surrender of France into the hands of her enemies. Fortunately for the Abbé, you then turned the conversation on to Jeanne d'Arc—and she made all well again. One of the children, out on the steps, exclaimed:

"How lovely the moon is tonight!" I went out. I knew that Marinette would come too. I heard her say in a low voice, "Wait for me." . . . She was wearing a "boa" round her neck.

The moon was rising full in the east. She expressed admiration of the long shadows cast by the elms on the grass. The farmworkers' cottages stood blind-eyed in the white radiance. A few dogs were barking. She asked me whether it was the moon that made the trees so motionless. She said that on such a night the whole of creation was but a torment to the lonely. "An empty stage!" she said. Everywhere, at this very moment, lips were pressed to lips, shoulders touched, heart responded to heart. I could distinctly see a tear quivering on her lashes. In the world's stillness her breathing was the only sign of life. . . . It was eager, it was hesitant. . . . You died in 1900, Marinette. What remains of you now? What remains of the body that was buried thirty years ago? I can remember the smell of it in the darkness. Perhaps, only if we have conquered the body can we believe in the body's resurrection. The punishment of those who have abused it is that they cannot even imagine that it will rise again.

I took her hand, as I might have taken the hand of an unhappy child, and, like a child, she leaned her head upon my shoulder. I received the gift of it merely because I happened to be there. The earth receives the fallen peach. Most human beings come together not as the result of any deliberate choice, but like trees that have grown side by side, their branches interlacing in the simple process of their growth.

But what made me infamous at that moment was that I thought of *you:* thought how I might be revenged on you, how

I might make use of Marinette to cause you suffering. It may have been for a fleeting second only, but it is true, nevertheless, that the idea of such a crime did enter my head. We took a few uncertain steps outside the zone of moonlight toward a clump of syringas and pomegranate trees. But Fate intervened. At that precise moment I heard steps in the lime walk—the walk that the Abbé Ardouin used every morning on his way to Mass. It was almost certainly he. . . . I thought of what he had said to me one evening—"You are a very good man." If only he could have read my heart at that moment! Perhaps the shame that overcame me at the thought was my salvation.

I led Marinette back into the light and made her sit down. I dried her eyes with my handkerchief and spoke to her as I might have spoken to Marie if she had fallen and I had picked her up under the limes. I pretended that I had not noticed the hint of an emotional disturbance in her tears and in the soft yielding of her body.

IX

Next morning she did not ride. I went into Bordeaux (I spent two days of each week there, even in vacation time, so as not to interrupt my consultations).

The Southern Express was standing in the station just as I was getting into the train to go back to Calèse, and great was my astonishment to see, through the window of a coach labeled *Biarritz,* Marinette in a gray tailor-made suit and without a veil. I remembered that a friend of hers had been pressing her for some time to join her at Saint-Jean-de-Luz. She was reading an illustrated paper and did not see the signs I made. That evening, when I mentioned the incident to you, you paid little attention to what you thought was a brief indulgence in liberty. You told me that, shortly after I had left, Marinette had received a telegram from her friend. You seemed surprised that I did not know this. Perhaps you had suspected us of having arranged to meet secretly in Bordeaux.

Besides, you had other things to think of. Little Marie had been sent to bed with a temperature. She had been suffering for some days from diarrhea, and you were uneasy. I will do you the justice to say that whenever any of the children were ill, nothing else mattered to you.

I want to pass quickly over what followed. After more than thirty years, it is only with an immense effort that I can bring my mind to dwell on it.

I know the substance of your charge against me. You had the effrontery to tell me to my face that I was against having a second opinion. I have no doubt that if we had called in Professor Arnozan he would have diagnosed what we took to be influenza as typhus. But cast your mind back. Once, but only once, you did say, "Mightn't it be as well to have Arnozan?" My reply to that was: "Dr. Aubrou tells me that he's been attending more than twenty cases of this type of influenza in the village. . . ." You didn't insist. You pretend now that you raised the point again next day, that you begged me to send a telegram to Arnozan. Had you done so I should have remembered it. That fact is, I've chewed old memories over and over through so many days and nights that I'm no longer sure what actually did happen. I know I've always been a miser about money, but not to the extent of trying to save expense where Marie's health was concerned. So it can't have been that, apart from the fact that Arnozan worked for the love of God and humanity. If I didn't call him in, the reason is that we were still convinced that it was simply a case of influenza that had "gone to the bowels." That ass Aubrou made Marie eat so as to keep up her strength. It was he who killed her, not I. You were entirely of my opinion, and if you say now that you urged me to call in Arnozan, you are lying. I was not responsible for Marie's death. That you should ever have accused me of such a thing is horrible. All the same, you *believe* I was; you've always believed it.

Oh, that relentless summer! the frenzy of the heat, the ferocious scraping of the grasshoppers. It was impossible to get any ice. All through those endless afternoons I sat wiping the sweat from her tiny face, which seemed to be a target for every fly within reach. Arnozan came at last, but too late. He changed the treatment, but by that time all hope of saving her was gone. It was probably only because of her delirium that she kept on saying—"for Papa!—for Papa!" . . . Do you remember the sound of her voice when she suddenly cried out, "Please, God, I am only a child . . ." and how she stopped, and went on, "No, I can stand it, I can . . ."? The Abbé gave her some water from Lourdes to drink. Our heads, yours and mine, came together above her exhausted body: our hands touched. When it was all over, you thought me callous.

Do you really want to know what was going on in my mind? I was thinking how strange it seemed that you, a Christian, should set such store by the *corpse*. You wouldn't leave it. We tried to get you to eat: we kept on telling you that you would need all your strength. But only by using force could we make you leave the room. You sat beside the bed, touching her cold forehead and her cheeks in a sort of fumbling way. Her hair, which still had life in it, you kissed, and now and again you slipped to your knees, not to pray, but so that you could press your face against the cold and rigid hands.

The Abbé Ardouin raised you up and spoke of how we must make ourselves like little children if we are to enter the kingdom of the Father. "She lives, she sees you, she is waiting for you." But you shook your head. The words did not even penetrate to your brain. Your faith was useless to you. You had thoughts for nothing but that flesh of your flesh, which was going to be laid in the earth and would soon know corruption. It was I, the unbeliever, who realized, as I looked at what was left of Marie, the full meaning of the word "remains." I was overwhelmed by a sense of departure, of absence. She was no longer there. *That* was not her: "Is it Marie that ye seek . . . ?—she is no longer here. . . ."

Later, you accused me of being quick to forget. Only *I* know what broke in me when I kissed her for the last time as she lay in her coffin. But what lay there was not really her. You held it against me that I did not accompany you to the cemetery, when you visited it almost every other day. "He never sets foot inside the place"—that was your constant complaint. "And yet," you would say, "she was the only person he seemed to have any feeling for. . . . The truth of the matter is—he's quite heartless. . . ."

Marinette came back for the funeral, but left again three days later. You were blinded by your grief and never saw the threat that was gathering in that direction. You even seemed relieved when your sister went away. Two months afterward, we heard of her engagement to a literary gent, a journalist whom she had met in Biarritz. It was too late, then, to put a spoke in her wheel. You showed yourself to be utterly unforgiving. It was as though some long-repressed hatred of Marinette had suddenly burst free. You didn't, you said, want to know the "creature"—who, as a matter of fact, was quite an ordinary sort of chap, pretty much like any other. His only crime was that he had deprived our children of a fortune. Not that he derived any benefit from it himself, since most of it went to Philipot's nephews.

But reason was never your strong suit. You were quite unscrupulous. I have never known anybody who could be so serenely unjust. God knows what peccadilloes you may have confessed in the secrecy of your heart—but there was certainly not one of the Beatitudes that you did not deny by the actions of your life. You thought nothing of accumulating false reasons against those you hated. You had never seen your sister's husband and knew nothing whatever about him, but that did not prevent you from saying: "She fell a victim to some sort of adventurer she met at Biarritz, a regular lounge-lizard type. . . ."

When the poor girl died in childbed (I don't want to judge you as harshly as you judged me in the matter of Marie), it wasn't only that you showed next to no regret. Events had proved you right. It had been bound to end like that. She had dug her own grave, and you had nothing with which to reproach yourself. You had done your duty. The wretched woman had known perfectly well that her family would always take her back if she made the slightest sign. You, at least, had had nothing to do with the business—that must have been a comforting thought! You had been firm—but at what a cost! "There are times when one has got to learn to trample on one's feelings!"

I don't want to be too hard on you. I realize that you behaved well to little Luc, Marinette's son, when there was no one to bother about him after your mother's death. You made yourself responsible for him during the holidays and went to see him once each winter in the school just outside Bayonne where he had been placed. "You did your duty"—such were your words—"even if his father didn't do *his*."

I have never told you how I came to meet Luc's father. It was in Bordeaux, in the September of 1914. I was trying to find a safe-deposit at a bank. The fugitives from Paris had taken them all. At long last, the manager of the Crédit Lyonnais notified me that one of his clients was returning to the capital and might, perhaps, consent to let me have his. When he told me his name, I realized that it was Luc's father. He was very far from being the monster you thought him. I tried in vain to recognize, in this man of thirty-eight, lean, hollow-cheeked, and worried to death by the constant threat of medical boards, the being whom, fourteen years earlier, I had seen at Marinette's funeral. I had a business talk with him. He expressed himself with the utmost frankness. He was living with a woman, but didn't want Luc to have anything to do with her. It was out of consideration for the boy that he had handed him over to the tender mercies of his grandmother. My poor Isa, if only you and the children had known what I offered him at that meeting! I can tell you now. My suggestion was that he should keep the safe-deposit in his own name, giving me power of attorney. I, for my part, was to leave all my liquid assets there, with a document stating that they were Luc's property. So long as I lived, he would have been powerless to touch them, but, after my death, could have taken possession without your knowing a thing. . . .

Obviously, I should have been putting myself and my fortune into his hands. How I must have hated you at that moment! But the man wouldn't play. He was too frightened. He spoke of his "honor."

How came it that I could have entertained such a mad idea? At the time I am speaking of, our children must have been within measurable distance of their thirties. They were married, were definitely on your side, were opposed to me on every conceivable issue. You were working in secret. I was the enemy. God knows you were not on particularly good terms with any of them, and especially not with Geneviève. Your grievance against her was that she left you out of everything, that she never asked your advice. But against me, you maintained a common front. Nevertheless, everything between us was conducted in a muted key, except on solemn occasions. For instance, there were terrible battles over the children's marriages. I set my face against giving anything in the nature of a dowry and insisted on an allowance in each case. I refused to render an account of my financial position to either of the families concerned and stuck to my point. I had all the cards in my hand. Hatred was my strong suit, hatred and love—the love that I felt for young Luc. And the families put up with me because they felt so sure that my fortune was immense.

My silence worried you. You wanted to know. Sometimes Geneviève tried to get on the soft side of me. I could hear the poor ungainly creature clumping along in her clogs a mile off! I often said to her, "You'll bless me when I'm dead," just for the pleasure of seeing the greedy glint in her eyes. She passed on those wonderful words of mine to you. The whole family was in a state of trance. And all the time, I was trying to find some way of leaving you nothing beyond what could not be concealed. I thought only of young Luc. I even played with the idea of mortgaging the land. . . .

But on one occasion I did let myself be taken in by your play-acting. It was the year after Marie's death. I was ill. Some of my symptoms were not unlike those of the disease that had carried off our little daughter. I hate being fussed over. I have a horror of doctors and drugs. You nagged me until I agreed to stay in bed and see Arnozan.

You nursed me devotedly—that goes without saying—but also with a certain uneasiness. Sometimes, when you asked me how I was feeling, I thought I heard a note of anxiety in your voice. When you felt my forehead, you did it much in the same way as you would have done if I had been your child. You wanted to sleep in my room. If I was restless in the night you got up and fetched me a drink. "She is really fond of me," I used to say to myself: "who *would* have thought it!—I suppose it's because of what I make!" But there I was wrong. You don't love money for its own sake. It's more likely that what was worrying you was the thought that my death would leave the children poorer. But it wasn't that either.

When Arnozan had finished examining me, you had a conversation with him out on the steps, and you raised your voice once or twice as you so often do. It's a habit that's always giving you away. "I want you to let it be known, doctor, that Marie died of typhoid. People are saying it was consumption because of what happened to my poor brothers. There's so much ill-nature in the world. Once an idea gets about, it has a way of persisting. I'm so terribly afraid of the harm that sort of talk might do to Hubert and Geneviève. If my husband had been seriously ill it might have given substance to that sort of gossip. For some days I felt very anxious about him—thinking of the children. One of his lungs, you know, was affected before his marriage. That's a matter of general knowledge. People do so love that sort of thing. Even if he had died of some infectious disease, they wouldn't have believed it any more than they did in the case of Marie. And my poor darlings would have been the ones to suffer. It used to make me wild to see how little care he took of himself! He wouldn't even stay in bed—as though he had only himself to think of! But he never worries about anybody else, not even the children! . . . Men like you, doctor, find it difficult to believe that people like him exist. You're just like the Abbé Ardouin—who never thinks evil of anybody. . . ."

I lay there in bed, laughing to myself, and when you came back you asked me what I was laughing at. "Oh, nothing," I said. It was a kind of private language of our own. "What are you laughing at?" one of us would say—"Oh, nothing." "What are you thinking about?"—"Oh, nothing."

X

I take up this narrative again after an attack that has kept me in your power for close on a month. When illness weakens me, the family circle closes about my bed. The whole lot of you are there, watching me.

On Sunday Phili came to keep me company. It was hot: I answered him in monosyllables. I lost the thread of my ideas . . . for how long I can't say. The sound of his voice woke me. I saw him there in the half-light with his ears pricked. His eyes were glittering like a wolf cub's. He was wearing a gold chain just above his wristwatch. His shirt was open, and his chest looked like a child's. I dozed off again. The creaking of his shoes roused me, and I lay watching him through half-closed eyes. He was feeling my jacket, just where the inside pocket is in which I keep my notecase. My heart was thumping, but I forced myself to lie still. Perhaps his suspicions were aroused: anyhow, he went back to his chair.

I pretended that I had just woken up and asked him whether I had been asleep for long.

"Only a few minutes, Grandpapa." I felt that terror that visits old men when they know that young eyes are watching them. Am I going mad? I got the idea that he was quite capable of killing me. Hubert once said that Phili would stick at nothing.

I want you to know, Isa, how wretched I have been. By the time you read these pages, it will be too late for you to show me pity, but I like to think that you may feel a little. I do not believe in the everlasting hellfire of your creed, but I do know what it is to be damned in this life, and outcast. I realize only too clearly that whatever road I choose I am bound to lose my way. All through my life I have chosen wrongly, I have never learned how to live—not in the sense that those of this world understand living. Of the art of life I have, quite literally, known nothing. I am in torment, Isa. The south wind is burning up the air. I am thirsty and have nothing with which to assuage my thirst but a lukewarm tap. I am the owner of millions, but am without so much as a glass of cold water to my name.

Phili's presence terrifies me. I think I put up with it only because he reminds me of somebody else, of that young Luc, our nephew, who would now be a man of over thirty. I have never denied your virtues, but he gave you no opportunity to show them. You never liked him. There was nothing

"Fondaudège" about Marinette's boy. He had jet-black eyes. His hair grew low over his forehead and swept back from his temples in what Hubert used to call a couple of "love locks." In that school at Bayonne where he was a boarder his reputation for work was bad. But that, you said, was no concern of yours. You had quite enough to do looking after him in the holidays. He took no interest in books. Though this countryside is poor in game, he managed to find something to kill every day, contriving to "get" the one and only hare that lurked, each year, in the trenched earth of the vineyard. I can see him still, holding the dead beast by the ears, its muzzle smeared with blood, and waving triumphantly to us as he tramped back between the growing grape shoots. I used to hear him starting out at dawn. I would open my window, and his clear young voice would call up to me through the mist: "Just off to take a look at my night lines."

He invariably looked me straight in the face. There was nothing shifty about his eyes. He wasn't frightened of me: the idea of being frightened of me never entered his head. If I happened to come home unexpectedly after a few days' absence and caught the smell of cigar smoke in the house, or found the carpet up in the drawing room with all the signs of a hastily interrupted party (I had only to turn my back for Geneviève and Hubert to provoke an "invasion"—in spite of my strict injunctions to the contrary—and you always aided and abetted their disobedience, because, you said, "one must return hospitality"), it was invariably Luc they sent to make their peace with me. The terror I inspired just made him laugh. "I went into the drawing room while they were dancing and called out, 'Here's Uncle, he's come by the shortcut!'—and, by Jove, you should have seen them hop it! Aunt Isa and Geneviève spirited the sandwiches away into the pantry! What a hullabaloo!"

That boy was the only person in the world I couldn't scare. Sometimes, when he set off on a day's fishing, I used to go down to the river with him. Usually, he could never keep still, was forever dashing about here, there, and everywhere, but on those occasions he was capable of standing perfectly motionless for hours on end, all eyes. It was exactly as though he had been turned into a tree: the slow, noiseless movements of his arm were like that of a swaying branch. Geneviève was perfectly right when she said that he would never be "literary." He couldn't be bothered to go out on the terrace at night to look at the moon. He was entirely without a feeling for nature, because he *was* nature, was wholly absorbed into it, was one of its forces, a living spring among its many springs.

I used to think of all the drama his young life had known—a dead mother, a father who was never mentioned in our presence, a lonely life in a remote school. Much less than all that would have sufficed to fill *me* with bitterness and hate. Everybody loved him, and that seemed strange to me, whom everybody loathed. Yes, everybody loved him—even I. He had a smile for all, including me—but not more for me than for the others.

His nature was purely instinctive, and what struck me more and more, as he grew older, was his purity, his unawareness of evil, his utter disregard of it. I don't mean to imply that our children weren't "good." Hubert, as you always said, was a model youth. In that respect, I must admit, your early training had borne fruit. I wonder whether, if Luc had lived into manhood, he would have remained so utterly untroubled. I never got the impression that, with him, purity was something he had been taught, something of which he was conscious. It had the limpid quality of water running over a stony bed. It glittered on him like the dew on grass. I dwell on this because it had a profound effect on me. Your parade of high principles, your hints, your expression of distaste, your pursed lips—these things never made me so truly aware of evil as did that boy, though I was not conscious of it at the time, nor for many years afterward. If, as you hold, humanity carries in its flesh the stigma of original sin, then, all I can say is that no living eye can ever have seen the mark in Luc. He had come from the hand of the potter uncracked and lovely. I felt myself, in comparison with him, deformed.

Is it accurate to say that I loved him like my own son? No, because what I loved in him was that complete absence of all trace of myself. I know only too well what of myself I have bequeathed to Hubert and Geneviève—sharpness of temper, the exorbitant value that they attach to material things, and a certain violence of contempt (in Geneviève's treatment of her husband, Alfred, there is a relentless quality that I recognize only too well). I could always feel quite sure that I should never bump up against myself in Luc.

During the rest of the year I scarcely thought of him. He spent Christmas and Easter with his father and returned to us only with the coming of the summer holidays. In October he migrated with the other birds.

Was he religious minded? You used to say: "Even in a young animal like Luc one can see the influence of the good Fathers. He never misses taking communion on Sundays. . . . I know, of course, that he hurries through his act of contrition, but, after all, no more is asked of any of us than we can give."

He never spoke to me about religion, even indirectly. His talk was always of the concrete. Sometimes when he pulled from his pocket a knife, a float, or a whistle for luring larks, his little rosary of black beads would fall to the ground. When that happened, he would hurriedly pick it up. But perhaps on Sunday mornings he did seem a little less scatterbrained than on other days, less evanescent, less imponderable, and as though charged with some unfamiliar current.

The links that bound me to Luc were many, but one of them may cause you some surprise. At times, on those Sunday mornings, I thought I could detect in the young fawn whose leapings were, for the moment, stilled, the brother of the little girl who had fallen asleep twelve years earlier—of our Marie. And yet, how different they were! She, you will remember, could never bear to see an insect crushed, and loved to line a hollow tree with moss and set in it a statue to the Virgin. All the same, in Marinette's son, in the boy whom you used to call "a little animal," I seemed to see Marie again: or, rather, what I felt was that the same fresh spring, which had bubbled up in her and then gone underground again, was once more gushing at my feet.

When the war broke out, Luc was not quite fifteen. Hubert was mobilized into the auxiliary forces. The medical boards to which he submitted with philosophic resignation, filled you with anxiety. For years his narrow chest had been a nightmare to you, but now your hopes were centered on it. When the deadliness of office work, and occasional jeers, made him eager to volunteer for active service (he really did try), you began to speak openly of what, for so long, you had been careful never to mention. "With your heredity . . ."—that was how you put it.

My poor Isa, don't be afraid. I'm not going to throw stones at you. You have never taken the slightest interest in me, have never really noticed me at all, and in those days you did so less even than usual. You had no idea of the mounting terror in me as winter followed winter. Luc's father was called up in one of the ministries, and we had the boy with us not only in the summer holidays, but at Christmas and Easter as well. The war filled him with enthusiasm. The only thing he was afraid of was that it might be over before he was eighteen. Formerly, he had never opened a book, but now he took to poring over maps and military manuals. He embarked methodically on a course of physical exercises. At sixteen he was already a full-grown man—and a tough one at that. He had no feelings to spare for the wounded and the dead. I gave him to read the grimmest accounts I could find of life in the trenches, but the picture he derived from them was of some terrible and magnificent form of sport in which all were not privileged to take a part. He would have to hurry up! How fearful he was of being too late! His idiot of a father had already given him written permission to offer himself as a volunteer, and this he carried in his pocket always. As the fatal day in January '18 approached, I followed with frightened concentration old Clemenceau's career, always on the watch for something to happen. I felt as must have felt those parents of men held prisoner, who used to watch for Robespierre's fall, hoping against hope that the tyrant would be laid low before their loved ones came to trial.

When Luc was under instruction in the training camp at Souges, you used to send him knitted mufflers and all sorts of little comforts, but you used to say things, my poor Isa, that made me feel like murder—for instance: "Of course it would be terrible if anything happened to the poor boy—but, at least, he wouldn't leave anyone behind him." . . . I know you didn't mean any harm. . . .

A day came when I realized that it was no longer any good hoping that the war might be over before Luc was called up. When the front was broken on the Chemin des Dames, he came to say good-bye, a full fortnight earlier than he had expected. Well, it couldn't be helped. . . . And now I must pluck up courage to tell you of an incident so horrible that it still wakes me at night and makes me cry aloud. On the day to which I have referred, I went into the study to fetch a leather belt that I had got the local saddler to make to my own specification. Then, I climbed on a stool and tried to pull toward me a plaster cast of the head of Demosthenes, which stood on top of the bookshelves. But I could not move it. It was full of gold coins that I had hidden there since the war began. I plunged my hand into all that gold, which represented for me what I most valued in the world, and began to stuff the leather belt with money. When I got down from the stool, the swollen snake, gorged with metal, was hanging round my neck and weighing me down.

Shyly I held it out to Luc. At first he did not grasp what it was that I was offering him.

"What on earth do you expect me to do with that, Uncle?"

"It may come in useful in billets, or if you're taken prisoner . . . or in other ways. With money you can do anything."

"Oh!" said he, with a laugh. "I've got quite enough to carry as it is. . . . You didn't really think, did you, that I'd load myself up with all that money? The first time I went into the line, I'd have had to bury it in the woods!"

"But, my dear boy, at the beginning of the war, everyone who had any gold took it with him."

"That's because they didn't know what they were in for, Uncle."

He was standing in the middle of the room. He had thrown the money belt on the sofa. Strong though he was, he looked terribly frail in his ill-fitting uniform. The collar was far too big for him, and his neck looked like a drummer boy's. His cropped hair had taken all character from his face. He had been made ready for death, decked for the sacrifice. He was just another item in the mass, without identity, anonymous, as good as vanished. For a moment he stared at the belt, then he raised his eyes to mine with an expression of mockery and contempt. All the same, he gave me a hug. We went down with him to the front door. He turned his head and shouted back: "Much better take all that to the Banque de France." By that time I could no longer see anything, but I heard you say, with a laugh:

"Don't be too sure of that! it's asking a lot of him!"

Somebody shut the door. I stood in the hall quite motionless. You said:

"You knew perfectly well, didn't you, that he wouldn't accept the money? It was a perfectly safe gesture on your part."

I remembered that the belt was still on the sofa. One of the servants might quite easily have found it there: one could never be sure. I hurried upstairs, looped it round my neck again, and emptied the contents back into the head of Demosthenes.

I scarcely noticed my mother's death, which took place a few days later. Her mind had been wandering for years, and she no longer lived with us. It is only now that I think of her every day, remember her as the mother of my childhood and young manhood. The picture of her in those last years has faded from my mind. Though I hate cemeteries, I still go, at times, to visit her grave. I used to take flowers, but I have given up doing that because I noticed that they were always stolen. The poor sneak the roses of the rich for the benefit of their own dead. I ought to have a railing put up, but everything's so expensive nowadays.

Luc has no grave. He just disappeared, was one of the "missing." I keep in my notecase the only card he had time to send me. It was one of the printed Field-Service affairs: "All well: have received your parcel. Love." The word *love* was in his own handwriting. That message at least I did get from my poor child.

XI

Tonight I woke, fighting for breath. I felt a compulsion to get up. I dragged myself to my chair and sat, reading over, to the accompaniment of a howling wind, the last few pages I had written. I was appalled by the light they shed on my deepest self. Before settling down to go on with them, I leaned for a while at the window. The gale had dropped. Calèse was wrapped in sleep. There was not so much as a breeze, and the sky was full of stars. Suddenly, about three o'clock, there was another squall. The sky rumbled, and heavy, icy drops began to fall. They rattled on the tiles so loudly that I feared they might be hail. I thought that my heart had stopped beating.

The grapes have barely "set." Next year's harvest covers all the slopes. But it seems that it may be with it as it is with those young animals that the hunter tethers and then leaves in darkness to attract the prowling beasts of prey. Clouds, heavy with thunder, are snuffling round the proffered vines.

But what do I care now about the grape harvest? I have nothing left to harvest in this world. The only thing left for me to do is to get to know myself a little better. Pay attention, Isa. After my death, among my papers, you will find a statement of my last wishes. They date from the months immediately following Marie's death, those months during which I was ill, and you were worried on account of the children. You will find, too, my profession of faith. It runs something like this: "Should I agree, at the moment of my death, to accept the ministrations of a priest, I herewith, while my mind remains clear, protest against the advantage that will have been taken of my weakening powers—physical as well as mental—to extort from me what my reason rejects." I owe you that confession. It is, on the contrary, when I study myself, as I have been doing for the past two months, with a closeness of attention that is stronger than my feeling of disgust, and when I feel my mind to be at its clearest, that the temptations of Christianity most torment me. It is then that I feel it impossible to deny that a way does exist in me that might lead me to your God. If I could reach the point of feeling satisfied with myself, I could fight this sense of pressure with more hope of success. If I could despise myself unreservedly, then the issue would be settled once and for all. But when a man is as hard as I am, when his heart, as in my case, has become dead wood, when he can inspire only hatred and create about himself nothing but a wasteland, then he has no defense against the onrush of hope. . . . I wonder if you really understand what I am getting at, Isa?

Perhaps it is not for you, not for the army of the just, that your God came into the world, if come he did, but for us. You have never known me, have never realized the kind of man I am. Do I seem less horrible to you, now that you have read these pages? You must surely see by this time that there does exist in me a secret string that Marie could touch merely by snuggling into my arms, or little Luc, when, returning from Mass on Sundays, he would sit down on the bench in front of the house and stare at the distant plain.

Don't please think that I am painting too pretty a picture of myself. I know my heart—it is a knot of vipers. They have almost squeezed the life out of it. They have beslavered it with their poison, but, underneath their squirming, it still beats. Impossible now to loosen the knot. I can fight free only by cutting it with a knife, by slashing it with a sword: *I am come to bring not peace but a sword.*

It may well be that tomorrow I shall deny what I here confess, just as, tonight, I have denied those final wishes that I confided to paper thirty years ago. I have seemed to hate, with a hatred for which I may yet make atonement, all that you profess: and I shall still go on hating those who call themselves Christians. But is it not because so many of them degrade hope and distort a Countenance, *that* Countenance, *that* Face? You will say that a man, heavy as I am with abominations, has no right to sit on them in judgment. But isn't there, Isa, in my very vileness something (I don't know what) that, more than all their virtues, resembles the Sign of your adoration? What I am writing here must seem to you nothing but an absurd blasphemy. But you must prove it to me. Why do you not speak to me? Why have you never spoken to me? Perhaps—who knows?—some word of yours might rend my heart. I feel tonight that even now it is not too late for us to start again. Suppose I don't wait until I am dead to let you see these pages? Suppose I beg you, in the name of your God, to persevere with them to the end? Suppose I wait until you have reached the last word? Suppose I saw you come into my room with tear-stained face and open arms? Suppose I asked your pardon? Suppose we knelt down, side by side, and prayed?

It seems as though the storm is over. The dawn stars are twinkling in the sky. I thought the rain had started again, but it was only the dripping of the trees. If I lie down again I shall have to fight for breath. I can't write any more. Now and again I drop my pen and let my head fall against the hard back of the chair.

A hiss like that of a wild beast, then a deafening din and a great glare filling all the sky. In the panic silence that followed, I heard the sound of fireworks on the hills, set off by the vine growers to scatter the clouds or resolve the hail to water. Rockets were leaping into the air from the darkness where shrouded Barsac and Sauterne were waiting in terror for the coming of the scourge. The bell of St. Vincent's, which keeps the hail away, has been ringing with might and main. The sound of it is like that of someone singing in the night because he is afraid. Suddenly, from the roof there came that noise as of a handful of flung pebbles . . . hailstones! Time was when I should have rushed to the window. I could hear the sound of shutters flung back, and your voice crying down to a man who was hurrying across the yard: "Is it serious?" . . . "'Tis all mixed with rain," he replied; "and that be lucky: but 'tis coming down proper hard." A frightened child has just run barefoot down the passage. I find myself, from force of habit, reckoning: "A hundred thousand francs gone west . . ."—but I have not stirred. Nothing, in the old days, could have kept me from rushing downstairs—one night they found me out among the vines, wearing my slippers, holding a candle, and bare-headed under the hail. Some profound peasant instinct had driven me out as though to fling myself upon the ground and cover the beaten vines with my body. But tonight I have become a stranger to all that was once best in me. Those restricting bonds have, at last, been loosened, by what or by whom I do not know. The cables have been cut, Isa, and I am adrift. What power is leading me on? Is it blind—or is it love? Perhaps it may be love. . . .

PART TWO

XII

What induced me to pack this notebook? What has this long drawn-out confession to do with me now? I have broken with my family forever. She for whom I laid myself bare in these pages can exist for me no longer. Why, then, resume the task? The answer to that question is, I suppose, that, though I did not know it at the time, the setting down of all my thoughts on paper brought me comfort and release. What a revelation of my state of mind those last lines contain, written on the night of the hailstorm! I must have been within measurable distance of madness. . . . No, no, I won't even mention that word: I mustn't, because they are quite capable of quoting any mention of it against me, should these pages ever fall into their hands. They are no longer addressed to anybody in particular, and, when I feel myself getting worse, I shall have to destroy them, unless, of course, I decide to leave them to the unknown son in search of whom I have come here to Paris. I longed to reveal the fact of

153

his existence to Isa in that passage that deals with my love affair of 1909. I was actually on the point of confessing that when my mistress ran away it was because she was with child and had made up her mind to find a hiding place in Paris.

I thought I was being very generous because I allowed mother and child six thousand francs a year before the war. It never occurred to me to increase the sum. If the two people I have found here are ground down and enslaved by sordid toil, the fault is mine. On the pretext that they live in this district, I am staying at a pension in the Rue Bréa. There is scarcely room, between the wardrobe and the bed, for me to write: and, oh! the din! In my days Montparnasse was quiet. Now it appears to be inhabited exclusively by lunatics who never go to bed! The family made considerably less noise on the front steps at Calèse that night when I saw with my own eyes and heard with my own ears . . . but what's the point of reviving that memory? . . . I suppose that by giving it shape and form I shall free my mind of an obsession, at least for a while. . . . After all, why should I destroy these pages? My son and heir is entitled to all the information about myself that I can give him, and this confession will, to some extent, fill out the gap that I have set between us ever since he was born.

We have had two meetings, and I can now, alas, make up my mind about him. He is not the kind of man to take the slightest interest in what I have written. How can a miserable junior clerk, a numskull who spends all his spare time betting on horses, hope to understand?

All that night in the train, between Bordeaux and Paris, I spent the time imagining his reproaches and formulating my defense. What a hold the tawdry conventions of novelists and playwrights have over one! I felt so sure of finding myself confronted by the bastard of fiction, all bitterness and noble sentiments! I endowed him, turn and turn about, with Luc's nobility and Phili's looks. I was ready for anything—except only that he would turn out to be the living image of myself! Are any fathers really pleased to be told that their sons are "just like" them?

I realized the full extent of my self-loathing when I was brought face-to-face with this pale image of myself. In Luc, I had loved a son who was utterly unlike me. In Robert's case, there is only one difference between us—he has shown himself to be quite incapable of passing even the simplest examination. He has tried again and again, but always with the same result: failure. His mother, who has worked herself to the bone, despises him for this lack of success. She can't help constantly referring to it. He hangs his head. He hates the idea of so much money being thrown down the drain. In that respect he is indeed my son! But the fortune I am bringing him is beyond the power of his miserable comprehension to grasp. It means nothing to him: he doesn't really believe in it. The truth of the matter is, both he and his mother are thoroughly frightened— "It's not legal . . . we might be caught."

This pale, flabby woman with the faded hair, this caricature of the girl I loved, just sat and stared at me when I went to see her (she still has beautiful eyes). "If I'd passed you in the street," she said, "I'd never have recognized you!" Should I have recognized her? I had steeled myself against possible reproaches, against her wish to be revenged for what had happened, against everything, in fact, except this dreary indifference. Embittered, worn down by eight hours a day at the typewriter, she lives in a constant dread of scandal. Years ago she ran foul of the law, and since then has had a morbid terror of it. I explained my whole scheme to them. The idea is that Robert should rent a safe-deposit in his own name, and that I should at once transfer to it such of my fortune as can be moved. He would give me power of attorney to have access to it, and take a solemn oath not to touch a penny of it till I am dead. Naturally, I should insist on his giving me a signed statement to the effect that everything in the safe-deposit belongs to me. I am not going to put myself in the hands of a complete stranger. But both mother and son have raised an objection. At my death, they say, the paper will be found. The fools don't trust me!

I have tried to make them realize that we should be perfectly safe in the hands of a country lawyer, some fellow like Bourru, who owes everything to me, and with whom I have done business for forty years. He is keeping, locked away, an envelope on which I have written: "Please burn on the day of my death," and I am quite sure he will burn it, with all its contents. Into that envelope I should put Robert's signed statement. I am the more certain that Bourru will burn the packet because there are in it certain documents that it is very much to his interest to see out of the way. But Robert and his mother are afraid that, once I am dead, Bourru won't burn anything and will start blackmailing them. The same idea, I confess, had occurred to me, and, to guard against it, I am prepared to put evidence into their hands that would be sufficient to send him to penal servitude. I should make it a condition that the paper must be burned in their presence, and that then, and then only, they give back to him the weapon with which I shall have provided them. What more can they want?

But they can't grasp it. They're too pigheaded. One is a fool, the other an imbecile. I am offering them millions, and instead of going down on their knees in gratitude—as I fully expected they would—they go on arguing and splitting hairs! . . . Even supposing the thing is a bit risky, surely the game is worth the candle? But no, they won't sign. "In the first place, the income-tax authorities might make difficulties."

The fact that I didn't slam the door in their faces proves how bitterly I hate the rest of my family. Incidentally, they're frightened of the family, too. "They'd smell a rat, they'd bring

an action against us. . . ." They've already got it firmly fixed in
their heads that my relations have warned the police, and that
I'm being watched. They won't see me except after dark, and in
odd, out-of-the-way places. Do they expect a man in my state
of health to sit up half the night and spend my life in taxis? I've
no reason to suppose that anybody at home is suspicious. This
isn't the first time I've taken a trip alone. They can't know that
I was present, though invisible, at the council of war they held
the other night at Calèse. In any case, they won't have got on
my trail yet. This time, nothing's going to keep me from reach-
ing my goal. The day Robert consents to play ball I can sleep in
peace. He's too great a coward to be careless.

It's the thirteenth of July tonight, and there's a band playing in the open air. Couples are dancing at the end of the Rue
Bréa. Oh, for the peace and quiet of Calèse! I remember my
last night there. In spite of doctor's orders I had taken a tablet
of veronal and had fallen into a deep sleep. I awoke with a start
and looked at my watch. It was one o'clock in the morning. I
could hear several voices, and that frightened me. I had left
the window open. There was no one in the courtyard nor in
the drawing room. I went into my dressing room, which looks
north and is on the same side of the house as the steps. It was
there that the family, contrary to habit, was making a night of
it. At that late hour they had no reason to believe they would

be overheard. The only windows on that side of the house are those of the various dressing rooms and of the corridor.

The night was still and warm. Every now and then there was a pause in the conversation, and I could hear Isa's rather wheezy breathing, and the sound of a match being struck. There was not enough breeze to rustle the leaves on the dark elms. I didn't dare lean out, but I could recognize my enemies by their voices and their laughter. They were not arguing. Isa or Geneviève would say something, and then there would be a prolonged silence. But all of a sudden, Hubert spoke. At once Phili flared up, and then they all started talking at once.

"Are you quite sure, Mamma, that the papers in his study safe are really of no value? Misers are always careless. Don't you remember all the money he wanted to give young Luc . . . where's he hidden that?"

"He realizes that I know the combination: it's 'Marie.' He never opens the safe except when he wants to look at an insurance policy or a tax return."

"But, Mamma, there might be some record of how much this money amounts to. . . ."

"There's nothing in the safe but papers relating to his house property; I'm sure of that."

"Don't you think all that's terribly significant?—I mean, doesn't it show that he's taken every possible precaution?"

There was a yawn from Phili: "What an old crocodile!" he muttered; "just my luck to hit on a crocodile like that!"

"If you want my opinion," said Geneviève, "you won't find anything in his safe-deposit at the Crédit Lyonnais either. What do you think, Janine?"

"But there are times, Mamma, when it really does look as though he's got a sort of feeling for you. Wasn't he ever nice to you when you were children? If not, that must have been because you didn't know how to get round him, because you weren't clever. You ought to have tried to appeal to his better nature and win him over. I'm sure I could have succeeded if he hadn't had such a horror of Phili."

Hubert broke in with a bitter comment: "There's no doubt your husband's insolence has cost us pretty dear."

I caught the sound of Phili's laugh and leaned forward a little. The flame of a cigarette lighter lit up for a moment his cupped hands, his flabby chin and thick lips.

"It didn't need me to set him against you!"

"That's not true: he hated us much less in the old days."

"Don't forget what Grandmamma told us, about how he behaved when the little girl died," went on Phili: "how he didn't seem to care and never set foot in the cemetery."

"That's going a bit too far, Phili: if ever he cared for anyone in the world it was for Marie."

But for this protest of Isa's, made in a faint and trembling voice, I could not have controlled myself. I sat down on a low chair and leaned forward, resting my head against the window-sill. Geneviève was speaking:

"If Marie had lived, nothing of all this would have happened. He would have been bound to watch over her interests."

"Oh, come! he'd have got his knife into her, as he has into everybody else! He's a monster and doesn't know what human feelings mean!"

Once again Isa protested:

"You mustn't talk about my husband like that, Phili, in front of me and his children! You do owe him *some* respect."

"Respect?"

I thought I heard him mutter something like—"If you think it's fun for me to have got mixed up with a family like this! . . ."

His mother-in-law broke in dryly:

"Nobody forced you!"

"Every kind of glittering expectation was dangled before my eyes. . . . Oh, now Janine's blubbering . . . what have I said that's so extraordinary?"

The sound of his voice faded away in a sort of exasperated grumble. I could hear nothing but the noise Janine made in blowing her nose. A voice that I could not identify murmured: "How bright the stars are!" St. Vincent's clock struck two.

"Time for bed, children."

Hubert protested that they couldn't separate before something had been decided. It was high time to act. Phili agreed. He didn't think I could last much longer, and once I was dead it would be too late. It was a pretty sure thing that I had taken steps.

"Children, children, what do you expect me to do? I've tried my best, and there's nothing more to be done."

"Oh yes there is," said Hubert; "You could . . ." What was he whispering? Just what I most wanted to know I couldn't hear. I gathered from the tone of Isa's voice that she was shocked, scandalized.

"No, I couldn't possibly agree to that. . . ."

"It's not a question of personal feelings, Mamma, but of saving our inheritance."

There were more vague murmurings, cut short by Isa:

"But that would be a terrible thing to do!"

"But, don't you see, you're playing his game, Grandmamma? He can't disinherit us unless you agree, and this is a case of silence giving consent. . . ."

"Janine, my dear, how can you!"

Poor Isa! She had spent endless nights sitting up with this squalling little brat, and had even taken her into her own room because her parents wanted to sleep and no nurse would put up with her. . . . There was an edge to Janine's voice that I wouldn't have let pass for a moment. She went on:

"I don't like saying things like this to you, Grand'ma, but it's my duty. . . ."

Her duty! that was the name she gave to the urgencies of her body, to the terror she felt at the idea of being abandoned by the scoundrel whose idiotic laugh now floated up to me.

Geneviève backed up her daughter. It was quite true, she said: weakness might so easily turn to complicity.

Isa sighed:

"Perhaps the best thing would be to write him a letter . . ."

"Oh, for heaven's sake, no letters!" Hubert protested. "Letters are always our undoing! I do hope, Mamma, that you haven't already written to him?"

She admitted that she had, just once or twice—"but nothing threatening or abusive." She was obviously embarrassed. I laughed to myself. Oh, yes, there had been letters all right, and I was taking good care of them. Two contained passages of pretty serious abuse, but the third was couched in almost affectionate terms, quite affectionate enough, anyhow, to make it certain that she would lose any suit for separation that those idiotic children might persuade her to bring.

The feeling of uneasiness was now general. It was just as when a dog starts growling, and the rest of the pack follow suit.

"Oh, don't say that you've written him any letters that might be dangerous to us, Grand'ma."

"I don't *think* I have, though I'm afraid there was one . . . I know that Bourru, the lawyer over at St. Vincent . . . I think my husband's got some hold over him (anyhow, he's a nasty creature, a hypocrite to boot) . . . did say that it was most unwise of me to have written. . . ."

"What was it you wrote? Nothing abusive, I do hope?"

"There was one in which I reproached him a little too violently after Marie's death, and another in 1909 referring to a liaison of his that was rather more than usually persistent. . . ."

Hubert groaned out something about it's being "very serious, extremely serious," but she tried to reassure him by adding that she had made everything all right since by expressing her regrets and admitting that she had been wrong. . . .

"That just about puts the lid on it! . . . so he knows he can't be dragged into court now! . . ."

"But, after all, why should you think he means to treat you all so badly?"

"You'd realize soon enough if you weren't completely blind. The dark mystery of his financial operations; the hints he drops; that remark he made to Bourru, in front of witnesses, when he said: 'They'll look pretty silly when the old man dies. . . .'"

They went on talking as though Isa had not been present. She struggled out of her armchair with a groan. She oughtn't, she said, to stay out after dark, with her rheumatism. The children did not so much as answer her. I heard the inattentive "good night's" they gave her without bothering to interrupt what they were saying. It was she who had to move round the circle distributing good-night kisses. They none of them budged. I thought it safer to lie down again in bed. I heard the sound of her heavy steps on the staircase. She came right up to my door. I could clearly catch the noise of her uneasy breathing. She put her candle down and opened the door. She came across and stood close to my bed, leaning over me, with the object, no doubt, of making quite sure that I was asleep. What a long time it seemed! I was afraid of giving myself away. Her breath was coming in little gasps. At last she went out and closed the door. As soon as I heard her bolt her own, I went back to my listening post in the dressing room.

The children were still there, but now they were talking in whispers. Much of what they said escaped me.

"Don't forget," observed Janine, "that he came of a different social class. . . . Phili, darling, you're coughing, *do* put on your overcoat."

"Actually, it's not his wife he most hates" (Geneviève now), "but us. What a fantastic situation—if you read of it in a novel you wouldn't believe it! It's not for us to judge our mother," she wound up, "but I do think she's been a bit too forgiving. . . ."

"Damn it all!" (Phili). "She can always get her marriage settlement back. Old man Fondaudège's canal shares must have gone up a good deal since '84!"

"B-but they've been . . . sold."

I recognized the hesitant tones, the hemming and the hawing, as coming from Geneviève's husband. Until that moment the wretched Alfred had not opened his lips. His wife cut him short. She spoke in the sharp, shrill voice that she keeps for him:

"You must be mad! The Suez Canal shares sold?"

Alfred explained how, in the May of that year, he had gone into his mother-in-law's room and found her signing some documents. She had said: "I'm told that now's the moment to sell. They're standing very high and will almost certainly drop."

"And you mean to say you never told us?" exclaimed Geneviève. "Really, I believe you must be half-witted! He actually made her sell the Suez?—is *that* what you're trying to explain? You just casually mention it as though it were the most natural thing in the world!"

"But, Geneviève, I thought your mother would tell you what she'd done. In any case, by the terms of her settlement, she remains mistress of her own property."

"That's all very well, but it's more than likely that he pocketed the profits of the sale! What's your opinion, Hubert? To think he never breathed a word—and that's the man I'm tied to for the rest of my life!"

At this point Janine told them to speak lower, so as not to wake her little girl. For the next few moments I heard scarcely a word. Then, once again, Hubert's voice rose above the general buzz.

"I've been thinking about what you were saying just now. . . . But, you know, we should never get her to agree, and even if we did manage to convince her, it would be a long, slow business. . . ."

"She might prefer it to a separation. Separation, you see, is bound to lead, sooner or later, to divorce, and that would involve a case of conscience. . . . Of course, what Phili proposes does sound a bit shocking at first, but after all, *we're* not going to have to say the word: it won't be for *us* to make the final decision. All we've got to do is to get the thing started. Nothing will happen unless the competent authorities think it necessary. . . ."

"Well, as I said before," remarked Olympe, "you'll all of you be going to a lot of trouble for nothing. . . ."

Hubert's wife must have been thoroughly outraged to raise her voice as she did. She maintained that I was a perfectly sensible man, a man of sound judgment. "I don't mind admitting," she said, "that we quite often agree about things, and that if you weren't forever butting in, I could do anything I liked with him. . . ."

Phili must have made some pretty insolent reply, though I couldn't hear what it was. They all laughed, as they always do when Olympe joins in. I caught a few disjointed phrases.

"He hasn't conducted a case for five years . . . hasn't been up to it."

"Wasn't that because of his heart?"

"His heart's bad *now,* but when he gave up practicing there was nothing particularly wrong with him. The real trouble was he was always getting at odds with his colleagues. There were quite often scenes when he was conducting a conference—I've got firsthand evidence of that. . . ."

I strained my ears, but it was no good. Phili and Hubert had drawn their chairs together. All that reached me was an indistinct murmur. Then, suddenly, there was another outburst from Olympe:

"He's the only one of the whole lot of you I can talk to about books, or discuss general ideas with, and you want . . ."

Phili said something in reply. I caught the word "looney." One of Hubert's sons-in-law, who scarcely ever says anything at all, gave a sort of a splutter:

"You might be at least decently polite to my mother-in-law. . . ."

Phili protested that he was only joking. Weren't they both of them playing the part of victims in this business? Hubert's son-in-law asserted, in a trembling voice, that he didn't look on himself as a victim, and that he'd married his wife for love, at which there was a chorus of "Same here!—Same here!—Same here!" Geneviève mockingly remarked to her husband:

"You'll be saying next, I suppose, that *you* married me without knowing how much my father was worth?—But *I* happen to remember that on the night we became engaged you whispered: 'What's the odds? It doesn't matter if he won't talk about it, we *know* it's enormous. . . .'"

There was a general burst of laughter, followed by a babble of voices. Once again it was Hubert who dominated the meeting. For a moment or two nobody interrupted him. It was only his final remark that I heard:

"The one thing that really matters in all this affair is justice and morality. We are defending our inheritance, the sacred rights of the family. . . ."

In the deep hush that comes before the dawn, I could hear more clearly:

"Have him watched? He's too well in with the police! I've proof of that—they'd put him wise . . ." (then, a few moments later) ". . . everyone knows he's as hard as nails and as greedy as you make 'em. I've even heard it whispered that he hasn't been all he should be in business . . . though, of course, no one's ever doubted his good sense and his judgment. . . ."

"Well, there's no denying that his feelings for us are inhuman, monstrous, and unnatural. . . ."

"But do you really think, Janine, my dear," said Alfred to his daughter, "that *that* would be sufficient to get him certified? . . ."

It had been beginning to dawn on me, and now I knew! I felt perfectly calm: certainty had brought a sense of peace. It was they who were the monsters, I who was the victim. The fact that Isa had been absent gave me pleasure. So long as she had been with them, she had, to some extent, protested. In her presence they had not dared to mention the plan that I had just overheard. Not that it terrified me. Poor fools!—as though I were the kind of man to let himself be put under restraint or shut away! Long before they so much as raised a finger, I could put Hubert in a hopeless position. He had no idea what a hold I had over him. As to Phili—there was a whole dossier about *him*. . . . I have never really seriously intended to make use of it and I shan't have to. It'll be quite enough if I show my teeth.

For the first time in my life I felt the satisfaction of being outdone in malevolence. I did not in the least want to be revenged on them, or, rather, the only vengeance I envisaged was to snatch from their grasp the inheritance over which they were hanging in a fever of impatience, and sweating with anxiety.

"A shooting star!" cried Phili: "I had no time to make a wish."

"One never does have time," said Janine. Her husband, with that childish gaiety that he has never lost, said:

"Whenever you see one you should cry 'millions'!"

"What an ass you are, Phili!"

They all got up. The garden chairs scraped on the gravel. I heard them shoot the bolts of the front door and the smothered laughter of Janine in the passage. One after the other the bedroom doors were shut. I had decided what to do. I had had no attack now for two months. There was nothing to keep me from going to Paris. As a rule, when I started on a trip I said nothing about it. But I did not want them to think I was running away. I spent the time until morning in going over the plans I had already made, dotting the i's and crossing the t's.

XIII

When I got up at midday, I had no feeling of fatigue. I put a call through to Bourru and he arrived after luncheon. For nearly three quarters of an hour we walked up and down under the limes. Isa, Geneviève, and Janine were watching us from a distance, and I thoroughly enjoyed the thought of how anxious they must be. What a pity that the men were all in Bordeaux! "Bourru," they were fond of saying, "is his evil influence"—that wretched, petty attorney who was more wholly in my power than any slave could have been! It was a sight for sore eyes to see the poor devil twisting and turning in his terror lest I might leave my heir some weapon that could be turned against him. "But," I told him, "don't you see, once you've burned the signed receipt, we'll hand everything over. . . ."

When he left, he made a profound bow to the ladies, who scarcely acknowledged it, and rode off on his squalid bicycle. I joined the three females and explained that I was leaving that evening for Paris. When Isa protested that I was much too ill to travel alone, I said:

"I've got to see about my investments. You may not believe it, but it's of you I'm thinking."

They looked at me uneasily. The note of irony in my voice gave me away. Janine, with a glance at her mother, plucked up courage to say:

"Grand'ma or Uncle Hubert could easily go instead. . . ."

"There's something in that, my dear . . . but, you see, I've always been in the habit of seeing to these things myself. I know it's very wrong of me, but I don't trust anybody."

"Not even your own children? Oh, Grand'pa!"

She stressed the word "Grand'pa" in a rather priggish way. Her coaxing manner was hard to resist. How exasperating that voice of hers could be—the same voice that I had heard the night before mingled with the others.

I gave vent to a laugh, that dangerous laugh of mine that makes me cough. It plainly terrified them. I shall never forget the look of exhaustion on poor Isa's face. They must have been at her already. Janine would probably return to the charge as soon as I had left them: "Don't let him go, Grand'ma! . . ."

But my wife was in no mood to attack. She was at the end of her tether, completely done up. I had heard her, a few days back, say to Geneviève: "I'd like to go to sleep and never wake up. . . ."

She produced a softening effect on me, just as my poor mother used to do. Worn out though she was, a broken-down old machine, good for nothing, the children were still trying to set her against me. Of course they were fond of her in their own way. They made her see the doctor and keep to a diet. . . .

As soon as her daughter and granddaughter moved away, she came up to me.

"I need some money . . ." she began hurriedly.

"Today's the tenth: I gave you your month's allowance on the first. . . ."

"I know, but I had to lend some of it to Janine. They're terribly hard up. I can save while we're at Calèse. I'll pay you back out of my August allowance."

I said it was no business of mine, but that I was certainly not going to keep that fellow Phili.

"I've got several bills outstanding, too, with the butcher and baker, for instance, look. . . ."

She took them out of her bag. I felt sorry for her and offered to write out checks for them. "In that way I shall know that the money won't go into anyone else's pocket." She agreed. I took out my checkbook and noticed that Janine and her mother in the rose garden were looking at us.

"I don't mind betting," I said, "that they think you're talking to me about something quite different."

Isa trembled. In a low voice she said: "About what?" At that moment I felt a tightening in my chest. I clutched at it with my two hands in a way that she knew only too well. She came close to me:

"Are you in pain?"

I clung to her arm for a moment. There, under the limes, we must have looked like an old married couple ending their lives after long years of happy union. "It's better now," I brought out. She must have thought that this was the moment to speak, a unique opportunity: but she had no strength left. I noticed that she, too, was struggling for breath. Ill though I was, I had put up a fight. She had surrendered, given in. She had nothing with which to fight.

She seemed to be looking for the right words, glancing furtively the while at her daughter and granddaughter, as though to draw courage from their proximity. In the face she turned to me I saw an indescribable weariness. There may have been something of pity in it, there certainly was something of shame. The children must have wounded her to the heart on that memorable night.

"I'm worried at the thought of you going off alone."

I said that should anything happen to me while I was away, it wouldn't be worth having me brought back here.

She begged me not to talk like that. I said: "It would be just a waste of money, Isa. Cemeteries are much of a muchness everywhere."

"I feel the same," she said. "They can bury me anywhere they like, for all I care. There was a time when I wanted to lie near Marie . . . but what is there left of her?"

Once again I realized that, for her, Marie was no more than dust and ashes. I dared not tell her that, for years past, I had felt my child to be alive, that I had, as it were, breathed her in, had been conscious of her as of a fresh breeze blowing through the darkness of my days.

Geneviève and Janine did not get much satisfaction from their spying. Isa seemed to be utterly exhausted. Was it that she realized at last the nothingness of what she had been fighting for all these years? Geneviève and Hubert, goaded by their own children, had set this old woman on to me, Isa Fondaudège, the young, sweet-scented girl of those nights at Bagnères.

For close on half a century we two had been enemies, and now, on this heavy afternoon, the enemies had suddenly become aware of the bond created, in spite of the long drawn-out struggle, by a shared old age. We might seem to hate one another, but, for all that, we had reached the same point in the road. There was nothing now beyond that promontory on which we stood awaiting death. Nothing, at least, for me. She had her God, or should have had. All the things to which she had clung with such bitter determination (and I, too, had clung with desperation) were fallen away; all the greedy desires that had stood between her and the Eternal Being. Could she see him now that there was nothing to impede her sight? No, there were still the demands and ambitions of her children. It was *their* greediness that now hung about her neck like a burden. She must begin all over again and be hard on their account. Worries about money, worries about health, schemes of ambition and of jealousy. There they all were in wait for her, like a schoolboy's exercise on which the master has written—"To be done again."

She turned her head and looked again toward the walk where Geneviève and Janine, armed with pruning clippers, were making a pretense of trimming the roses. From the bench on which I had sat down to recover my breath, I watched my wife move away. She was hanging her head like a child in fear of a scolding. The excessive heat of the sun was sure portent of a storm. She was walking with the gait of those to whom walking is painful. I could almost hear her groaning, "Oh, my poor legs!" Husbands and wives of long standing never hate one another as much as they think they do.

By this time she had reached the children. Obviously, they were blaming her for something. All of a sudden, I saw her coming back toward me red in the face and out of breath. She sat down beside me with a groan.

"This stormy weather tires me so! My blood pressure's very high these days. . . . Listen, Louis, there's something I'm worried about. . . . How have you reinvested the money from those Suez Canal shares that were part of my settlement? I know there were some other documents you got me to sign. . . ."

I gave her the figure of the enormous profit I had realized for her by selling just before the market broke and explained that I had put the proceeds into debentures.

"Your settlement has been breeding, Isa. Even allowing for the depreciation of the franc, you'll be amazed. Everything's in your name at the Westminster Bank, your original settlement, and the profits. . . . It's nothing to do with the children . . . you can be quite easy in your mind. My money is my own, and what that money has produced, but what was yours is yours still. You can reassure those angels of unselfishness over there."

Suddenly she gripped my arm:

"Why do you hate them so, Louis? Why do you hate your own flesh and blood?"

"It's you who hate me, or rather, it's my children. *You* merely ignore me, except when I get on your nerves or frighten you. . . ."

"You might add 'or when I torture you.' Don't you know that I have suffered abominably at times?"

"Oh come! you had eyes for nobody but the children. . . ."

"I had to cling to them. What had I got but them?"—and, in a lower voice, she added: "You know perfectly well that you neglected me, that you were unfaithful to me from the very first year of our marriage."

"My poor Isa, you can't make me believe that my occasional wild oats really meant anything to you . . . as a young wife you may, perhaps, have been a bit hurt in your pride, but . . ."

"You really sound as though you mean what you say. . . . Why, you never even noticed whether I was there or not! . . ."

A feeling of hope set me trembling—which was strange, when you come to think that we were talking of emotions long since dead—of the hope I had entertained, unknown to myself, forty years before, that perhaps I was loved. . . . But no, it was asking too much that I should believe that now. . . .

"You never spoke a word, you never uttered a sound. All you needed was the children."

She hid her face in her two hands. I was more conscious than I had ever been before of their prominent veins and discolored patches.

"My children! Do you realize that when we took to having separate rooms, I never, for years and years, had one of them to sleep with me, even when they were ill, because I was always half expecting, half hoping, that you would come!"

Her old woman's hands were wet with tears. This was Isa. I alone could see, in that thickened, almost crippled body, the young girl with "a devotion to white" whom I had known on a road in the valley of the Lys.

"It's disgraceful, it's ridiculous, at my age, to recall such memories . . . ridiculous, especially . . . Please forgive me, Louis."

I stared at the vines and said nothing. I was a prey to sudden doubt. Is it possible that a man can live for nearly half a century noticing one side only of the person who shares his life? Can it be that, from long habit, he picks and chooses from among her gestures and her words, keeping for use only those that feed his grievances and perpetuate his resentments? There is a fatal tendency in all of us to simplify others, to eliminate in them everything that might soften the indictment, give some human lineaments to the caricature that our hatred craves in order to justify itself. . . . Perhaps Isa noticed my uneasiness; I wonder. At any rate, she was a shade too quick about scoring her next point.

"Say you won't go tonight!"

I fancied that I caught the familiar glint in her eye that always tells me when she thinks she's "got" me. I pretended to be surprised and answered that I saw no reason for putting off my journey. We went back to the house together. Because of my heart we did not climb the slope by the elms, but took the lime walk, which leads round to the far side. In spite of everything, I still felt doubtful and uneasy. What if I didn't go? What if I gave Isa what I have written? . . . What . . .

She laid her hand on my shoulder. How many years was it since she had last done that?

The lime walk ends in front of the house, on the north side.

"Cazau never tidies up the garden chairs. . . ."

I gave them an absentminded glance. The empty chairs were still set in a close circle. Those who had occupied them had felt it necessary to draw them together so that they could keep their voices low. I could see heel marks on the ground. The butts of Phili's special brand of cigarette were lying all over the place. Only a night or two ago the enemy had camped there, taking council under the stars, discussing in my own home, in front of the trees that my father had planted, the advisability of putting me under restraint, of having me shut away. Once, in the dark hours, in a moment of self-deprecation, I had compared my heart to a knot of vipers. How wrong I had been! The knot of vipers was outside myself! On that night of plotting they had wriggled free of me and twined themselves into a tangle, into a hideous circle at the foot of these steps. Their slime was still visible on the ground.

You shall have that money back, Isa, I thought: the money of yours that I have set to breed, but nothing more, nothing else. I would even find some way of keeping the estate out of their hands. I would sell Calèse and the stretch of heath. Everything that had come to me from my family should go to that unknown son of mine, to the boy whom I was to see in two days' time.

Whatever he might turn out to be, at least he had one great advantage—he didn't know you. He had taken no part in your plotting. He had been brought up far from my sight and could not hate me, or, if he did, the object of his hatred was an abstract being having no connection with myself.

Angrily I broke free and hurried up the steps, forgetful of my old man's heart. Isa called after me: "Louis!" But I did not even turn my head.

XIV

I could not sleep, so I dressed and went out into the street. In order to reach the Boulevard Montparnasse I had to force my way through the dancing couples. In the old days, even a dyed-in-the-wool Republican such as I was avoided the July 14 merrymaking. No respectable citizen would have dreamed of taking part in the festivities of the street. But this evening, in the Rue Bréa, and in front of the Rotonde, the men who were dancing were far from being rowdies. There was nothing vicious about them. For the most part they were well-set-up, bare-headed young fellows. Some of them wore short-sleeved, open-necked shirts. Very few of the girls were tarts. They clung to the wheels of such taxis as broke up the dancing, but gaily and without hostility. A young man who had jostled me by accident cried: "Way for the noble ancient!" I moved between a double row of radiant faces. "Not sleepy, Grand'pa?" a chap with a dark complexion and hair growing low over his forehead flung at me. Luc would have learned to laugh just like that, to dance in the streets, and I, who had never known

185

what it meant to relax and enjoy myself, would have caught
the secret from my poor boy. He would have reveled in the
scene, would have taken his fill of it, and he wouldn't have
wanted for money. . . . Fill? . . . it was with earth his mouth
was filled now. . . . So ran my thoughts, while, conscious of
the old familiar tightness in my chest, I sat in front of a café
with the fun going on all round me.

And then, quite suddenly, in the crowd that swarmed along
the pavement, I saw myself. It was Robert in the company of
a rather seedy individual. How I hate Robert's long legs, his
stocky body, so like my own, and his absence of neck! In him
my defects are exaggerated. *My* face is long, but his is like a
horse's—the face of a hunchback; and his voice is a hunchback's too.

I called to him. He broke away from his companion and
looked about him uneasily.

"Not here," he said; "meet me on the right-hand pavement
of the Rue Campagne-Première."

I pointed out that we could not be more effectively concealed than at the heart of this hubbub. He let himself be persuaded, took leave of his friend, and sat down at my table.

He had a sporting paper in his hand. To break the silence
I tried to talk about horses. I'd got into the way of it with old
Fondaudège, years ago. I told Robert how, when my father-
in-law betted, he always took all sorts of considerations into

account—not only the animal's pedigree to the third and fourth generation, but the ground conditions that suited it best and . . . He interrupted me:

"I get my tips at Dermas's" (Dermas is the name of the draper's shop in the Rue des Petits-Champs, where he's fetched up high and dry in a job).

The only thing he cared about was winning. Horses as horses bored him.

"Give me bicycles every time!" he said, and his eyes sparkled.

"Soon it'll be motors," I said.

"That's what you think!"

He moistened his thumb, took out a slip of cigarette paper, and rolled himself a cigarette. Silence once more descended between us. I asked whether the slump had made itself felt in his business. He replied that some of the staff had got the sack, but that he was safe enough. Not once did his talk stray outside the narrow circle of his personal concerns. It was into the lap of this nitwit that millions were to fall! Suppose I give it all to charity, I thought; or distribute it piecemeal? . . . No, for in either case *they* would have me put away. By will, then?—impossible to exceed the legally stipulated proportion. Oh, Luc, if only you were alive! . . . True, he wouldn't have accepted it, but I could have found some way of enriching him without his knowledge . . . by settling money, for instance, on the woman he might have loved. . . .

"Look here, sir. . . ."

Robert stroked his chin. His hand was red, the fingers spatulate.

". . . I've been thinking things over. What if that lawyer fellow, Bourru, should happen to die before we had burned the paper? . . ."

"Well, his son would succeed him, and the weapon I've given you against the father could, should the occasion arise, be used against the son."

Robert went on stroking his chin. I made no attempt to say more, so fully occupied was I with the feeling of tightness, with the agonizing constriction, in my chest.

"And again, what if Bourru burns the paper and I hand over what you'd given me to make him act proper? What's to stop him from going to your family and saying, 'I know where the dough is, and I'm ready to sell the secret—so much for giving you the lowdown, and a bit extra if you get your hands on it'—making it a condition that his name shan't be mentioned? . . . *He'd* be in the clear. There'd be an inquiry, and it'd come out as I really was your son, and that since your death Mother and I had been blowing it. . . . And we should either have to make a correct tax return or keep the whole thing dark."

He was expressing himself with precision. His mind was no longer sluggish. It had been slow in getting started, but now there was no holding it. The dominating instinct in this wretched counter jumper was peasant caution, peasant mistrust, and a horror of taking risks. He wasn't going to leave anything to chance. No doubt he would have preferred a hundred thousand francs in cash to the danger involved in having to conceal so vast a fortune.

I waited until my heart felt easier and the tightness had loosened. Then:

"There's something in what you say," I replied, "and I'll do what you want. You needn't sign anything. I'll trust you. As a matter of fact it would be perfectly easy for me to prove that the money is mine. Not that it really matters, because in six months, or a year at most, I shall be dead."

He made no gesture of protest. The commonplace that anyone else might have uttered was quite beyond him; not that he was more callous than other young men of his age, but simply that he had been badly brought up.

"That might work," he said.

He chewed my suggestion for a few moments and then continued:

"I'd have to look in now and again at the safe-deposit, even with you alive, just so's the bank people'd get to know my face. I might go and get some of the money for you when you wanted it."

"If it comes to that, I've got several safe-deposits abroad. If you'd rather, if you believe it would be less risky . . ."

"What, leave Paris! . . . what do *you* think!"

I pointed out that he could go on living in Paris and take an occasional trip when necessary. He asked whether my fortune was in securities or cash.

"I'd rather you gave me some sort of paper, something like you being of sound mind had left everything to me . . . just in case anything leaked out and I was accused of theft—one never knows. Besides, my conscience would be easier. . . ."

He stopped speaking, bought some peanuts, and started to eat them voraciously, as though he were hungry. Suddenly:

"What's your family done to you?" he asked.

"Take what I offer," I said dryly, "and don't be inquisitive."

A little color showed in his flabby cheeks. His smile was of the uncomfortable, self-conscious kind that he probably assumed when he was being hauled over the coals by his employer. It revealed the strong, pointed teeth that were the only good feature in his otherwise unpleasing face.

He went on shelling peanuts without saying anything more. There was nothing in his expression to show that he was in the least dazzled. Obviously, his imagination was getting to work. I had stumbled on the one person incapable of seeing anything in this marvelous windfall but the very small risks involved. But dazzled was just what I wanted him to be. . . .

"Haven't you got a girl?" I asked him point-blank. "You could marry her and live in solid, respectable comfort."

He made a vague gesture and shook his head with a hang-dog expression. I pressed my point.

"You could marry anybody you like. If there's any girl who seems out of your reach . . ."

He pricked up his ears at that, and, for the first time, I saw a glimmer of excitement in his eyes.

"I could marry Mademoiselle Brugère!"

"And who is Mademoiselle Brugère?"

"I was only joking. She's one of the heads at Dermas's. Proper stuck-up—won't so much as look at me; doesn't even know I exist. I say, that's an idea!"

I assured him that with a twentieth part of my fortune he could marry any "head" in Paris.

"Mademoiselle Brugère!" he said again. Then, with a shrug, "No, that's too much to expect!"

My chest was hurting. I signed to the waiter. It was then that Robert did a most surprising thing.

"No, look here, it's the least I can do. . . ."

I put my money back in my pocket with a feeling of satisfaction. We got up. The musicians were packing their instruments. The festoons of electric lights had been extinguished. There was no longer any reason why Robert should be afraid of being seen with me.

"I'll walk back with you," he said. I asked him to go slowly because of my heart. I was surprised that he did nothing to hasten the execution of our plans. I told him that if I died in the night he would lose a fortune. He showed complete indifference. All I had done was to throw him out of his stride. He was about my own height. Would he ever manage to look like a gentleman? This son and heir of mine was a poor creature! I tried to give an intimate turn to the conversation. I told him that I was filled with remorse to think that I had left him and his mother to their own resources. This seemed to surprise him. He thought it "very handsome" of me to have made them an allowance. "There's lots as wouldn't have done that." Then he said something quite horrible: "After all, you weren't the first. . . ." Obviously, he had no illusions about his mother!

When we reached my door he said:

"I've got an idea . . . what about my taking a job that would keep me hanging round the Stock Exchange? That'd explain my good luck, wouldn't it?"

"You watch your step," I said; "you'd very soon lose everything."

He stared at the pavement in a preoccupied manner. "I was thinking about the income-tax people. . . . What if the collector started making inquiries?"

"But this is a cash transaction, an anonymous fortune tucked away in a safe-deposit that no one but you in all the world would have the right to open. . . ."

"Oh, I know all about that, still . . ."

I was out of all patience and slammed the door in his face.

XV

A fly is buzzing against the window. I can see the slope of the hill. It looks numbed and lifeless. The wind is moaning and driving a mass of sagging cloud before it. Its shadow lies across the plain. This deathlike stillness means that everything is waiting for the first rumble of the thunder. On just such a day of summer, thirty years ago, Marie said: "The vines are frightened. . . ." I have reopened this notebook. Yes, no doubt of it, the handwriting is mine. I examine the letters closely. I can see under each line the mark made by the nail of my little finger. I will tell the story to the end. I know now for whom it is intended. This confession had to be set down in black and white, but many pages of it I shall have to suppress, because the reading of them would be more than they could bear. Even I can't look through them without a pause. Every now and again I break off and hide my face in my hands. Here is the portrait of a man, of a man among other men. This is I. You may spew me forth, but that doesn't alter the fact that I exist.

On that night of July 13/14, after leaving Robert, I was barely strong enough to undress myself and lie down on my bed. It was as though a huge weight were crushing the life out of my body. All the same, I did not die. The window was open . . . had my room been on the fifth floor . . . but it was on the first, and if I had jumped I should probably not have been killed. It was that probability alone that kept me from trying. . . . I could scarcely stretch out my hand for the pills that usually bring me relief.

At dawn someone did at last answer my bell. A local doctor came along and gave me an injection, as a result of which I was able to breathe normally again. He told me that I was to make no movement of any kind. As the result of extreme pain one becomes as submissive as a young child. There was not the slightest danger of my budging. I was no longer distressed by the ugliness, by the disgusting smell, of the room and the furniture, or by the noise of that stormy July 14. Nothing distressed me now because I was no longer in pain. To be free from pain was all I asked. Robert came to see me in the evening but did not repeat the visit. His mother sat with me for two hours on her way home from the office, did me a few small services, and brought me my mail from the *poste restante* (no letter from the family).

I made no complaint and was very docile. I drank every-thing the doctor had prescribed. When I spoke of my plan, she changed the subject. "There's no hurry," she kept on say-ing. I sighed. "But there is," I said; "and the proof of that is here"—pointing to my chest.

"My mother's attacks were worse than yours, and she lived to be almost eighty. . . ."

One morning I felt better than I had done for a long while. I was very hungry. The food in my pension was uneatable. I was seized by a sudden desire to lunch at a little restaurant on the Boulevard Saint-Germain where I knew the cooking was good. The size of the bill there caused me less astonishment and anger than in most of the squalid eating places I usually frequented in my terror of spending too much money.

The taxi put me down at the corner of the Rue de Rennes. I took a few steps to test my strength. All was well. It was barely noon. I decided to have a bottle of Vichy at the Deux Magots. I found a seat inside, on the settee that runs along the wall, and gazed absent-mindedly out of the window at the boulevard.

My heart gave a little jump. Just outside, separated from me by no more than the thickness of the glass, I saw a fa-miliar vision of narrow shoulders, bald patch, grizzled nape, and undistinguished, projecting ears. . . . It was Hubert, peer-ing so nearsightedly at a paper that it was almost touching his nose. Obviously, he had not seen me come in. The beating of my sick heart quietened down. A horrible joy possessed me. I was spying on him, and he did not know that I was there!

It was difficult to imagine Hubert anywhere but in one of the fashionable cafés of the Grands Boulevards. What was he doing in this part of the town? His presence there was certainly not accidental. I had only to wait, having paid for my Vichy, so as to be free to get up and go out should it be necessary.

It was clear that he was waiting for somebody. He looked at his watch. I thought I knew who it was who would worm his way to him between the tables and was almost disappointed when I saw Geneviève's husband get out of a taxi. Alfred was wearing a straw hat cocked over one ear. When he was away from his wife, this fat little man in his forties reverted to type. His provincial dandyism was in striking contrast to Hubert's dark clothes. Hubert, said Isa, always dressed "like a Fondaudège."

Alfred took off his hat and mopped his shining forehead. He ordered an aperitif and swallowed it at a gulp. His brother-in-law was already on his feet, consulting his watch. I made ready to follow them. No doubt they would take a taxi. I would do the same and try to follow them, by no means an easy thing to do. But even to have got wind of their presence was something gained. I waited until they were on the curb before leaving my retreat. They did not, however, hail a cab, but crossed the square and made toward Saint-Germain-des-Prés, talking all the while. I was surprised and gratified to see them enter the church. A detective who watches a thief walking straight into a trap could not have had a more delicious emotion than the one that made me catch my breath. I took my time. They might have looked behind them, and, though my son is near-sighted, my son-in-law has extremely good eyes. In spite of my impatience, I waited for two good minutes on the pavement. Only then did I enter the porch in their wake.

It was a little after noon. I moved carefully up the almost empty nave but soon realized that the objects of my search were not there. It occurred to me for a moment that they might have seen me, that they had come into the church in order to throw me off the scent and had left it again by one of the doors in the side aisles. I retraced my steps and went into one of the transepts—the one on the right, being careful to conceal myself behind the enormous pillars. Suddenly, in the darkest part of the apse, I saw them against the light. They were sitting on two chairs, and between them was a third person, a person with humble, drooping shoulders, whose presence there in no way surprised me. It was the same individual whom, a while back, I had expected to see gliding toward my legitimate son between the tables. It was my other son, that miserable worm, Robert.

I had foreseen this treachery, but from weariness or laziness had not given it much thought. From the moment of our first meeting I had realized that this lily-livered creature had no stomach for the fight, and that his mother, haunted by memories of the law, would advise him to come to terms with the family and sell his secret for what he could get. I looked at the back of his idiotic head. He was firmly wedged between the two solid citizens, one of whom, Alfred, was what is commonly called a "good sort" (though with a keen eye to his own interests, even if he was inclined to take the short view—and, as a matter of fact, he found the short view pretty remunerative), while the other, my charming Hubert, was as sharp as you make 'em, and had just that air of arrogant authority (his legacy from me) against which Robert would be powerless. I looked at them from my pillar, much as one might look at a spider busy with a fly, when one has made up one's mind to kill both fly and spider. Robert's head drooped more and more. He had probably begun by saying "Fifty-fifty," secure in the belief that he held all the cards. But merely by making himself known to them, the poor fool had put himself in their hands and couldn't do anything but throw up the sponge. Watching the unequal battle, which I alone knew to be vain and futile, I felt like a god preparing to crush these miserable insects with my powerful hand, to stamp these twined snakes into the ground. I laughed.

Only ten minutes were necessary to reduce Robert to silence. Hubert was displaying a fine eloquence and was, no doubt, issuing his orders. The victim was expressing his agreement with brief movements of the head, while his servile back grew rounder and rounder. Alfred, lolling as though in an armchair, with his right foot resting on his left knee, had tilted his seat and thrown his head backward, so that I got an upside-down view of his flabby, bilious, black-bearded face.

At last they got up. I followed them, still taking great care not to be seen. They were walking slowly. Robert was between them with hanging head, and I half expected to see handcuffs on his wrists. His great red hands were kneading a soft felt hat of dirty gray. I had thought that nothing in the world would ever surprise me again, but I was wrong. Alfred and Robert made straight for the door, but Hubert dipped his fingers in the holy water stoup, turned toward the high altar, and made a flamboyant sign of the cross.

I was in no hurry now. I could afford to be calm. There was no point in following them. I knew that that evening, or the next day, Robert would at last urge me to carry out my plans. What should be my attitude? I had plenty of time in which to think about that. I was beginning to feel tired and sat down. What was uppermost in my mind at the moment, dominating everything else, was a feeling of irritation at Hubert's pious gesture. A young girl in the row in front of me, decently dressed and with no particular claim to looks, put a cardboard hatbox on the ground beside her and knelt. I had a side view of her. Her head was slightly bent, and her eyes were fixed on the same distant little door that Hubert, his family duty done, had just so gravely saluted. She was smiling faintly and was quite motionless. Two seminarists came in next. One of them, tall and very thin, reminded me of the Abbé Ardouin; the other was short and had a chubby face. They made their genuflection side by side and, like the girl, seemed stricken into immobility. I looked at what they were looking at and tried to see what they were seeing. There's nothing here, I said to myself, but silence, coolness, and the smell of old, sunless stones. Once again the face of the little workgirl held my attention. Her eyes were shut now. Their lids, with their long lashes, reminded me of Marie's as I had seen them on her deathbed. I could feel, almost within reach of my hand, and at the same time infinitely distant, the presence of an unknown world of goodness. Isa had often said to me: "You never see anything but evil—you find it every-where. . . ." That was true . . . and yet, it was not true at all.

XVI

I had my luncheon. My mind felt relaxed and almost gay. I had not felt so well for a long time. It was as though Robert's treachery, far from upsetting my plans, had given them a helping hand. A man of my age, I thought, who has been living under sentence of death for years, does not seek elaborate reasons for his changes of mood. They are organic. The myth of Prometheus means that all the sorrows of the world have their seat in the liver. But it needs a brave man to face so humble a truth. I was conscious of no physical discomfort. I digested my underdone steak without the slightest difficulty. I was glad it was so large because that meant I shouldn't have to spend money on another course. I would just have some cheese, which is both nourishing and cheap.

How should I behave to Robert? I must train my guns now on a new target. But I could not concentrate my mind. Besides, why burden myself with a plan? I should be better advised to trust to the inspiration of the moment. I dared not admit to myself that I was thoroughly looking forward to the fun of playing, like a cat, with this dim little field mouse. Robert wasn't within miles of suspecting that I had smelt a rat. . . . Am I cruel? Yes, I suppose I am, but no more so than anybody else, than all the other men in the world, than women, than children, than all except those (I thought of the little workgirl whom I had seen in Saint-Germain-des-Prés) who are in the service of the Lamb.

I took a taxi back to the Rue Bréa and lay down on my bed. The students who formed the main clientele of the house were away on holiday. I rested in peace and quiet. The fact that the top half of the door was glazed, though a grubby half-curtain concealed the panes, removed all sense of privacy. Several small pieces of wooden molding belonging to the "Renaissance" style bedstead had come unstuck and lay, carefully gathered together, in a gilded bronze "tidy" that stood on the mantelpiece. The wallpaper, designed to imitate watered silk, was disfigured by a number of spreading damp stains. Even with the windows open, the room was filled with a smell from the pretentious, red-marble-topped commode. A cloth, with a mustard-colored ground, covered the table. I found the general effect pleasing. It seemed to sum up the whole of human ugliness and ostentation.

I was awakened by the rustling of a skirt. Robert's mother was sitting by my bed. The first thing I noticed about her was her smile. Her obsequious attitude would have sufficed to put me on my guard, even if I had known nothing, and to warn me that I had been betrayed. There is a particular species of kindliness that always goes with treachery. I returned the smile and told her that I was feeling better. Twenty years before, her nose had not been so big. In those days, too, her large mouth had been adorned by a handsome set of teeth, which Robert had inherited. But today her smile revealed a "plate." She must have been walking fast, and the sour smell of her body battled successfully with the emanations from the marble-topped commode. I begged her to open the window wider. She did so and then came back, still smiling. Now that I was feeling well, she said, Robert was entirely at my disposal for the "business in hand." Tomorrow, Saturday, he would be free from midday on. I reminded her that the banks are closed on Saturday afternoons. In that case, she decided, he had better ask for some time off on Monday morning. There wouldn't be any difficulty about his getting it. Besides, there was no longer any need for him to keep on the right side of his employers. She seemed surprised when I insisted that Robert should stick to his present job for a few weeks longer. When she took leave of me, she said that she would come again with her son next day to see me. I begged her to let him pay his visit unaccompanied. I wanted, I said, to have a little talk with him, so that I might get to know him better. . . . The poor fool made no attempt to disguise her anxiety. She was pretty obviously afraid that her son would give himself away. But when I adopt a certain tone of voice, no one thinks of questioning my decision. I had no doubt that it was she who had urged Robert to come to terms with my family. I knew that frightened, uncomfortable young man too well by this time not to realize that he must be feeling very uneasy in the part he had agreed to play.

When the poor fool entered the room next morning, I saw at once that I had underrated the effect of the situation on him. It was obvious, from the appearance of his eyes, that he had not slept, and he seemed quite unable to look me in the face. I made him sit down and told him that I thought him looking far from well. I was affectionate, almost tender, in my manner. I described, with the eloquence of a practiced lawyer, the perspectives of happiness now opening before him. I drew a picture of the house and park I was going to buy, in his name, at Saint-Germain. It was to be furnished throughout in "period" style. There would be a pond well stocked with fish, a garage for four cars, as well as many other "features" that I improvised as I went along. When I spoke about a car, and suggested one of the biggest American makes, he was like a man in mortal agony. Obviously, he had promised not to accept a penny of my money during my lifetime.

"All your troubles are over," I said. "There is nothing for you to do now but to sign the deed of purchase. I have already arranged to hand over to you on Monday a sufficient number of securities to bring you in an income of a hundred thousand francs a year. That will keep you going. But the bulk of my liquid capital is in Amsterdam. We must go there together the week after next so as to get everything straightened out. . . . Is there anything wrong, Robert?"

"I . . . I . . . won't touch a penny during your lifetime," he stammered. ". . . I shouldn't like to . . . I don't want to deprive you of anything. Please don't insist. . . . It'd only make me feel awful!"

He was leaning against the wardrobe, his left elbow supported in his right hand, and biting his nails. I gave him the look that opposing counsel have learned to dread. In just such a way had I been used to fix my victim in the box, keeping my eyes riveted on him until he collapsed into the arms of the attendant police officer.

Actually, I forgave him. I felt that a burden had been lifted from my shoulders. How frightful to have had to end my days in the company of such a worm! I didn't hate him—merely, as it were, dropped him in the ash can. All the same, I could not resist the temptation to have a little more fun with him.

"I must say, Robert, your feelings do you credit. How charming of you to want to wait until I am dead! But I am not going to accept such a sacrifice. Everything shall be yours on Monday. By the end of next week a large part of my fortune will be in your name. No," I went on dryly (he had begun to protest), "not another word. I have made my offer and it's up to you to take it or leave it."

He still refused to meet my eyes. He needed, he said, a few days in which to think things over—by which, of course, the poor idiot meant to write to Bordeaux for orders.

"Your attitude surprises me, Robert. It really is very odd."

I thought I was looking at him more kindly, but my expression is apt to be a good deal fiercer than the feelings that inspire it. In a perfectly expressionless voice, Robert muttered:

"Why are you staring at me like that?"

I could not help imitating him. "Why am I staring at you like this? I might equally well ask why you can't look me in the face."

Those who are accustomed to being loved instinctively make all the gestures, and say all the things, most likely to win over their interlocutors. I, on the other hand, have grown so used to being hated and to frightening people, that my eyes, my brows, my voice, and my laugh automatically become the servants of this detestable gift of mine, so that they deliver their message even before I mean them to. The poor lad was twisting and turning under a gaze that I had thought to make sympathetic: but the more I laughed, the more ominous did my gaiety seem to him.

Much in the manner of a slaughterman giving the coup de grâce to an animal, I fired a point-blank question at him:

"How much did they offer you?"

I had used the second-person singular, and the effect of this, whether I liked it or not, was to give to my words a tone not so much of friendliness as of contempt.

"Who d'you mean?" he stammered.

He was clearly prey to an almost superstitious terror.

"The two gentlemen," I said; "the fat one and the thin one . . . yes, the thin one and the fat one."

I wanted to get the whole thing over and done with. The idea of prolonging the scene gave me the horrors (as when one can't bring oneself to crush a centipede under one's boot). "Come, don't take it so hard," I said; "I've forgiven you."

"*I* didn't want to do it . . . it was . . ." I put my hand over his mouth. I couldn't have borne to hear him accuse his mother.

"Ssh! No names! . . . How much *did* they offer you?—a million?—five hundred thousand?—less than that? Oh, surely not!—three hundred?—two hundred?"

"Not any sum down at all, but a regular allowance. That was what tempted us: it gives us a greater feeling of security. Twelve thousand francs a year."

"Starting from today?"

"No, from when they come into their inheritance. . . . They hadn't foreseen that you'd want to put everything in my name now, at once. . . . But is it too late? . . . Of course, they might sue us . . . unless we could keep the whole thing on the q.t. . . . Oh, what a fool I've been! I deserve everything that's coming to me!"

He sat on the bed, shedding squalid tears. One of his hands hung down, red and enormous.

"After all, I *am* your son," he whined; "don't let me down."

With a clumsy movement he tried to put his arm round my neck. I freed myself—but not roughly. I went over to the window and, without turning round, said:

"From the first of August you will receive a monthly sum of fifteen hundred francs. I shall take immediate steps to see that this amount is paid to you for life. Should you predecease your mother, it will revert to her. My family must never know that I got wind of the little plot hatched in Saint-Germain-des-Prés" (the name of the church made him jump), "and I need scarcely point out that the least indiscretion on your part will mean that you lose everything. All I ask in return is that you shall keep me informed of anything they may be planning against me."

He knew now that nothing escaped me and realized precisely what any future treachery would cost him. I made it quite plain that I wished never to see him or his mother again. They must write to me, *poste restante,* at the usual office.

"When are your accomplices of Saint-Germain-des-Prés leaving Paris?"

He assured me that they had taken the late train on the previous night. He made a great show of gratitude and of promises for the future, but I cut him short. He was, no doubt, flabbergasted by what had happened. A fantastic God, moving in a mysterious way, whom he had betrayed, had seized him, let him go, and picked him out of the abyss into which he had fallen. . . . He shut his eyes and went limp. Squirming like a mongrel cur, his ears flattened to his head, he cringingly took the bone I had flung to him and made off.

Just as he was going out of the door, a thought occurred to him. How, he asked, would he receive this allowance? Through what channel?

"You will receive it," I said dryly. "I always keep my promises. The rest does not concern you."

With his hand on the latch, he still hesitated.

"I'd rather have it in the form of a life-insurance policy, or something like that, taken out with a good, reliable firm. . . . I should feel easier in my mind . . . I wouldn't have to worry . . ."

With sudden violence I wrenched open the door that he was holding ajar and pushed him into the passage.

XVII

I leaned against the mantelpiece and mechanically counted the scraps of varnished wood in the "tidy."

For years I had dreamed of this unknown son of mine. Never, in the whole course of my wretched existence, had I lost the feeling that he was there. In some sport of the earth there lived a child born of my body whom I might one day find again, who might, perhaps, at some distant date, bring me comfort. That he was of humble condition served to tighten the bonds between us. I had liked to think that he resembled my legitimate son in nothing. I had endowed him in my mind with simplicity and strength of affection, two qualities that are by no means rare among the common people. And now, after all these years, I had played my last card. There was nothing to be hoped from him, nor from any living person. There was nothing left for me to do but curl up and turn my face to the wall. For forty years I had cheated myself into believing that I could accept the fact of hatred—both of the hatred I inspired and the hatred that I felt. But, like other human beings, I had cherished a hope and assuaged my hunger as best I could, waiting until I should be driven back on my last reserves. That moment had come, and it was all over.

I could not even look forward to the horrible pleasure of scheming how best to disinherit those who had wished me ill. Robert had put them on the scent, and, sooner or later, they would discover my hoards, even the ones that did not stand in my own name. Think of some other way? . . . Oh, if only I could go on living, could have time enough in which to spend everything and *then* die . . . leaving behind me not even enough to pay for a pauper's funeral! But all my life long I had saved. For years I had satisfied my lust for "putting by." How, at my age, could I learn to be a spendthrift? Besides, thought I, the children have got their eyes on me. Anything of that sort I might do would merely put a dangerous weapon into their hands. . . . I should have to ruin myself secretly, by driblets. . . .

But alas! I shouldn't know how! I was quite incapable of losing my money. If only it were possible to stuff my grave with it, to return, earth to earth and dust to dust, clasping in my arms my gold, my notes, my shares! If only I could give the lie to those who preach that, when we die, we must leave the goods of this world behind us!

There was, of course, "Charity." Good works are trapdoors opening into depths that can swallow everything. Why not send anonymous gifts to the Relief Committee, to the Little

Sisters of the Poor? Why not, at this fag end of my life, begin to think of others, of those who were not my enemies? But the horror of growing old consists in this, that one's age is the sum total of one's life, and not one figure of it can we change. It has taken me sixty years—I thought—to "create" this old man now dying of hatred. I am what I am. I should have to become somebody else. . . . Oh God! . . . Oh God . . . if only you existed! . . .

It grew dark, and a maid came in to turn down my bed. But she did not close the shutters. I lay down in the half-light. I dozed, in spite of the noise in the street and the glare of the lamps. Every now and again I returned to full consciousness for a brief moment, as one does on a journey when the train comes to a stop. Then, once more, I dropped off. Though I did not feel any worse, I got the idea that I had only to stay as I was and wait patiently until my sleep should become eternal. I still had to make arrangements for the promised allowance to be paid regularly to Robert. I wanted, too, to look in at the *poste restante,* since there was nobody now to do that for me. For the last three days I had not read my mail. One of the most ineradicable of human beliefs is that *some* day a mysterious letter will turn up. What better proof could there be that hope springs eternal in the human breast? We are none of us without it.

It was this preoccupation with the idea of letters that got me out of bed next day, about noon, and sent me off to the post office. It was raining. I was without an umbrella and kept close to the walls. My appearance aroused curiosity. People began to look round at me. What's so odd about me?—d'you take me for a lunatic? . . . If you do, you mustn't let on—my children might take advantage of a thing like that! Don't stare at me so! I'm just like everybody else—except that my children hate me and that I ought to take steps to protect myself from them. But that doesn't mean I'm mad. There are times when I am under the influence of all the drugs that an angina patient has to take. Yes, I *do* talk to myself, but that's because I am always *by* myself. Conversation is a necessity of all human creatures. What is there so extraordinary in the words and gestures of a lonely old man?

The packet I was given contained some printed matter, some letters from the bank, and three telegrams. They probably had to do with stock-exchange transactions that it had been impossible to put through. I delayed opening them until I should be seated in a cheap eating house. . . . Several builder's laborers, looking like Pierrots of varying ages, were seated at a long table eating their not very generous portions, drinking their liters, and scarcely speaking a word. They had been working in the rain all morning. At half-past one they would start again. It was the end of July. The stations were full of holiday-makers. . . . Would they have understood anything of the torment seething in my mind?—Of course they would: how could an old lawyer doubt it? My first case had had to do with children who had gone to law in some quarrel about looking after their father. The wretched man went to one or other of them every three months, only to be received with curses. The one point on which he had found himself in agreement with his sons was in calling loudly on death to bring them all release. Many was the form in which I had witnessed this drama of the old father obstinately refusing, year after year, to hand over the money bags, and then, finally, letting himself be wheedled out of his rights, only to die of overwork and hunger at the hands of his children. Oh, yes, the emaciated laborer with the gnarled hands, seated only a few feet from me, and slowly mumbling his bread between toothless gums, would surely know all about that.

No one, in these days, shows any surprise at the sight of a well-dressed old man in a cheap eating house. I cut up a piece of pallid rabbit and amused myself by watching the raindrops running together on the windowpane. I spelled out the name of the proprietor upside down. In feeling for my handkerchief, I came on the packet of letters. I put on my spectacles and opened one of the telegrams at random. "Mother's funeral tomorrow 23 July nine St. Louis church." It was dated that morning. The other two, sent off the evening before, must have followed one another at a few hours' interval. One of them said: "Mother desperately ill return." The other: "Mother dead. . . ." All three were signed "Hubert."

I crumpled up the telegrams and went on eating, my mind preoccupied with the thought that, somehow, I should have to muster up sufficient strength to take the night train. For several minutes I was concerned with nothing else. Then another feeling began to emerge—a feeling of amazement that I should have survived Isa. It had long been an understood thing that I was under sentence of death. Neither I, nor anybody else, had doubted for a moment that I should be the first to go. Plans, intrigues, plots—all had been centered on the days immediately following my death, which could not now be long delayed. I had been as certain of that as any member of my family, had always seen my wife in the character of a widow, encumbered by crape when she went to open my safe. No astronomical disaster could have caused me more surprise—or uneasiness— than this death. Automatically, the businessman side of me began to take stock of the situation, began to wonder how it could be used to advantage against my enemies. Such were my feelings until the train actually started.

It was only then that my imagination began to take a hand. For the first time I conjured up a vision of Isa as she must have looked in her bed on the previous day, and on the day before that. I saw the whole scene—her room at Calèse (I did not know then that she had died in Bordeaux). "Putting her into her coffin," I murmured to myself and yielded to a cowardly feeling of relief. What would have been my attitude had I been there? How should I have behaved under the watchful and hostile eyes of my children? That problem no longer arose. Furthermore, the fact that I should have to go straight to bed as soon as I arrived would settle every difficulty of that kind. There could be no question of my being at the funeral. Only a moment ago I had made an effort to go to the lavatory and had had to give it up. This evidence of my weakness did not frighten me. Now that Isa was gone, I no longer lived in hourly expectation of my end. My turn had gone by. But I *was* afraid of having an attack, the more so since I was alone in the carriage. I should be met at the station (I had sent a telegram) no doubt by Hubert.

But it was not Hubert who was waiting for me. What a relief it was to see Alfred standing there with his fat face showing all the marks of a sleepless night! The sight of me seemed to frighten him. I could not manage to get into the car unaided and had to take his arm. We drove in the gloom of a rainy Bordeaux morning through a district given over to slaughterhouses and schools. There was no need for me to talk. Alfred went into the smallest details. He described the exact spot in the public gardens where Isa had collapsed (in front of a clump

of palms just before one gets to the greenhouses), the chemist's
shop into which she had been taken, the difficulty they had
had in getting her heavy body upstairs to her room on the
first floor, the blood letting, the tapping. . . . She had been
fully conscious all night, though she was suffering from cere-
bral hemorrhage. She had kept on asking for me by means of
signs and had fallen asleep just as the priest arrived with the
consecrated oils. . . . "But she had taken communion the day
before. . . ."

Alfred wanted to drop me at the front door (which was
already draped in black) and hurry home, explaining that he
had barely time in which to get dressed for the ceremony. But
he had to resign himself to the necessity of helping me out of
the car. He gave me his arm up the first few steps. I did not
recognize the hall. In the dim interior great stands of candles
were burning round a massed bank of flowers. I blinked my
eyes. I felt lost, as one sometimes does in dreams. There were
two motionless nuns. They must have been provided by the
undertaker along with the other fittings. Behind this hotchpotch of fabrics, flowers, and lights, the familiar staircase, with
its shabby carpet, climbed into the region of everyday life.

Hubert came down. He was in evening dress and looked
very correct. He held out his hand to me and said something,
but his voice seemed to come from very far away. I tried to
answer, but failed to make a sound. His face drew closer and

became enormous. Then I lost consciousness. I learned later that my fainting fit lasted for a bare three minutes. I came to myself in what had once been my waiting room in the days when I was still practicing at the bar. There was the sharp prick of smelling salts in my nose. I recognized Geneviève's voice: "He's coming round." I opened my eyes. They were all there, bending over me. Their faces seemed different—red, puffy, and some of them with a greenish tinge. Janine, more robust than her mother, had the appearance of being her contemporary rather than her child. Hubert's face, in particular, showed the effects of tears. He had the same ugly, pitiful look as when, a child, he had been taken by Isa on her lap, and she had said, "The poor little mite's really unhappy. . . ." Only Phili appeared to be completely unchanged. Wearing the dress suit that he had dragged through all the night haunts of Paris and Berlin, he looked at me with the customary expression of bored indifference on his handsome face. He might have been just off to a party or, rather, just back from one, drunk and slovenly, for he had not yet tied his tie. Behind him I could make out a number of anonymous veiled women, who must have been Olympe and her daughters. Other shirt fronts gleamed in the half-light.

Geneviève held a glass to my lips, and I gulped down some of its contents. I told her that I was feeling better. In a gentle, kindly voice she asked whether I would like to go to bed at once. I said the first thing that came into my mind:

"I should so much have liked to go with her to the end, not having been here to say good-bye."

I repeated the phrase, like an actor seeking the correct inflection—"not having been here to say good-bye . . ."—and the flat words, serving no purpose beyond that of saving appearances. They had come to me only because they belonged to the part I was playing in the funeral ceremony, and suddenly awoke in me, with a sudden jerk, the very feeling of which they were the expression. It was as though I had told myself something that, till then, I had not realized. I should never again see my wife. There could never, now, be an explanation between us. She would never read these pages. Things would remain for all eternity in exactly the same state in which they had been when I left Calèse. We could not start afresh, wipe the slate clean, and try again. She had died without knowing me, without understanding that there was more in me than the monster, the tormentor, she thought me to be, that behind the mask there did exist a totally different man. Even if I had arrived at the last moment, even though no word had passed between us, she would have seen the tears that were now running down my face and would have died in the knowledge of my despair.

Only my children, speechless with astonishment, were witnesses of the scene. Probably, in the whole course of their lives, they had never seen me cry. The old surly, terrifying face, the Medusa's head at which they had none of them been able to look, had undergone a metamorphosis, had become simply that of a human being.

I heard a voice (it was probably Janine's):

"If only you hadn't gone away! Why did you?" Yes, why, indeed, had I gone? But I *could* have got back in time had the telegrams not been addressed to the *poste restante,* but delivered to me at the Rue Bréa. Hubert was foolish enough to add:

"Going away like that, without leaving an address . . . how could we possibly guess?"

A thought, till then vague in my mind, became, on a sudden, crystal clear. Pressing with my two hands on the arms of the chair, I struggled to my feet, trembling with anger, and shouted in his face the one word—"Liar!"

He was taken aback. "Papa!" he stammered, "you must be mad!"

But I went on: "Yes, you're liars, the whole lot of you. You knew my address perfectly well. I dare you to tell me to my face that you didn't!"

He protested feebly: "But how could we have known it?"

"You were in touch with somebody very close to me . . . you can't deny that, you know you can't!"

The whole family stared at me in a sort of petrified silence. Hubert shook his head like a child caught out in an untruth.

"You didn't give him much for his treachery: you weren't exactly generous. Twelve thousand francs a year in return for a fortune isn't much!"

I laughed and laughed until I was caught in a fit of coughing. They could none of them find anything to say. Phili muttered in a low voice: "Dirty trick. . . ."

I went on with what I had been saying, though I lowered my voice in deference to a gesture of appeal from Hubert, who was striving in vain to get a word in:

"You were the cause of my not coming back. You were being kept informed of my every movement; but I mustn't be allowed to know that. If you had sent me a telegram addressed to the Rue Bréa, I should realize at once that I had been betrayed. Nothing in the world would have induced you to take such a step, not even the prayers of your dying mother. No doubt you felt sorry, but you were cold and calculating. . . ."

All this I said to them, and other things still more horrible. Hubert begged his sister to intervene. "Make him stop! Make him stop! Somebody will hear him!" he said in a choking voice. Geneviève put her arm round my shoulders and made me sit down again.

"Not now, Father; not now. We'll talk about all that later when we're not so upset. I beg you, in the name of her who is still with us . . ."

Hubert's face was livid. He put a finger to his lips. The chief undertaker's man came in with a list of the pallbearers. I took a few steps. I did not want any of their supporting arms. I stumbled, and they drew aside to let me pass. I was able to cross the threshold of the mortuary chapel and squat down on a prie-dieu.

Hubert and Geneviève followed me. Each taking an arm, they led me away, and I made no effort to resist. They got me upstairs with considerable difficulty. One of the nuns agreed to keep an eye on me during the ceremony. Hubert, before leaving, with a great show of ignoring what had just passed between us, asked me whether he had done right in arranging for the president of the bar council to be one of the pallbearers. I turned away to the streaming window and said nothing.

Already there was a sound of many feet. The whole town would come to sign the visitors' book. On the Fondaudège side there were innumerable connections, and on mine, the bar, the bank, and the world of business. . . . I was conscious of a lightness of heart. I felt like a man who has just been acquitted of a crime, whose innocence has been declared to the world. I had convicted my children of lying, and they had made no attempt to deny their responsibility. While the whole house was echoing to the sound of feet—as though some strange ball without music was in progress—I forced myself to concentrate my thoughts upon their guilt. It was they alone who had prevented me from hearing Isa's last farewell. I stuck spurs deep into my ancient hatred, but, like a foundered horse, it would not respond. Perhaps the reason lay in my physical prostration, or in my satisfaction at the knowledge that I had had the last word. I cannot be sure.

I could no longer hear the singsong of the priest's voice. The sounds of the funeral died away, and a silence as deep as that of Calèse filled the huge house. Isa had emptied it of its inhabitants. Behind her corpse she trailed the paraphernalia of her home. No one was left within its walls but I and the nun, who was finishing, at my bedside, the telling of her beads, which she had begun beside the bier.

The silence made me sensitive once more to the fact of eternal separation, to that departure from which there is no return. Again I felt a tightness round my heart because now it was too late, and all was over between us. Propped up against the pillows of my bed, that I might breathe the more easily, I looked round at the Louis XIII furniture that we had chosen in Bardie's shop at the time of our engagement. It had been hers until she inherited her mother's. This bed it was, this melancholy bed, that had been the silent witness of our bitter wordlessness.

Hubert and Geneviève came in alone. The others had stayed outside in the passage. I realized that they could not get used to the sight of my tears. They stood beside my pillow, the brother, a bizarre figure dressed for the evening at midday, the sister, a mound of black picked out by a white handkerchief, and her veil thrown back to reveal a round and puffy face. Grief had unmasked us all, and we did not recognize one another.

They were worried about my health. Geneviève said:

"Almost everybody was at the cemetery: she was much beloved."

I asked them about the day before her stroke.

"She wasn't feeling well. She may, I think, have had a presentiment, because the day before she was due to go to Bordeaux, she spent hours in her bedroom, burning piles of letters. We thought the chimney must be on fire."

I broke in. A sudden idea had occurred to me. . . . Why hadn't I thought of it before?

"Geneviève, do you think my going away had anything to do with it?"

She answered with a satisfied air that, no doubt, "it had been a blow."

"But you didn't tell her, didn't keep her informed of what you had discovered?"

She shot a questioning glance at her brother: ought she to seem to understand? I must have presented an odd appearance at that moment, for, certainly, they seemed very much afraid. While Geneviève helped to prop me up in bed, Hubert hurriedly replied that his mother had been taken ill more than ten days after my departure, and that they had decided, throughout that period, not to include her in their melancholy discussions. Was he speaking the truth? In tremulous tones, he added:

"If we had yielded to the temptation of mentioning to her the uneasiness we were feeling, then, indeed, the prime responsibility would be ours."

He half turned away, and I could see his shoulders moving convulsively. Somebody pushed the door open and asked whether they were *ever* going to have something to eat. I heard Phili's voice: "Well, I can't help it, can I, if I'm starving?". . . Geneviève asked me through her tears what I would like for luncheon. Hubert said that he would come back after the meal, and that we must have everything out, once and for all, if I felt strong enough to listen. I nodded my agreement.

When they had left the room, the good sister helped me to get up. I was able to take a bath, dress myself, and drink a cup of beef tea. If there was to be a discussion I did not want to play the part of a sick man to be dealt with gently and protected.

On their return I was a very different person from the old gentleman who had aroused their compassion. I had taken the necessary drugs and was sitting upright. I felt less congested, as I always do when I leave my bed.

Hubert had changed into a day suit, but Geneviève was swathed in an old dressing gown belonging to her mother.

"I've nothing black to wear," she said. They sat down facing me. After a few conversational phrases:

"I've thought a good deal about this," Hubert began.

He had carefully prepared his speech and addressed me as though I had been a meeting of shareholders. He weighed each word and seemed anxious to avoid any show of anger.

"While I was sitting by Mamma, I scrupulously examined my conscience. I made a great effort to alter my point of view and to put myself in your place. We had regarded you as a father whose fixed idea was to disinherit his children, and that, to my mind, makes our behavior legitimate, or, at least, excusable. But we have given you a certain advantage over us by the violence with which we fought our cause, and by . . ."

He seemed to be looking for the right word. I murmured, very quietly, "and by your cowardly plots."

His cheeks showed a patch of color. Geneviève at once reacted:

"Why 'cowardly'? You're in a much stronger position than we are. . . ."

"Oh, come! . . . a very sick old man against a pack of healthy young animals!"

"In a family like ours," said Hubert, "a very sick old man is distinctly privileged. He never leaves his room; he can be constantly on the watch; he has nothing to do but observe the habits of his children and take advantage of them. He can make his plans undisturbed and arrange his moves at leisure. He knows all there is to be known about those round him, while they know nothing whatever about him. He has reconnoitered the best vantage points for listening . . ." (here I could not help smiling, and they smiled too). "Yes," Hubert went on, "the members of a family are always lacking in prudence. They argue, they raise their voices. In a very short while everyone is shouting without realizing it. They rely too much on the thickness of the walls in an old house, oblivious of the fact that the floors are flimsy, and that there are always open windows to be reckoned with. . . ."

These allusions had the effect of, to some extent, diminishing the tension between us. It was Hubert who first brought the conversation back to its serious level.

"I see now that we must have seemed blameworthy. It would be easy enough for me to plead legitimate self-defense, but I want to avoid anything that might embitter this discussion. It is no part of my intention to name the aggressor in this wretched quarrel. I am even prepared to plead guilty. But you must realize . . ."

He had got up and was wiping the lenses of his spectacles. The eyes blinked in his worn and harassed face.

". . . You must realize that I was fighting for the honor, for the very existence, of my children. It is impossible for you to imagine the situation in which we find ourselves. You belong to

a different century. You have lived your life in a fabulous period
when a careful man could plan his future on a basis of safe investments. Oh, I know that you are fully aware of what is happening
in the world, that you saw the storm coming before anybody
else did, that you realized in time . . . but that was because you
had retired from active business, because you were, if I may say
so, an onlooker. You could judge the situation quite coolly; you
dominated it, you were not, as I am, up to the ears in it. . . . The
awakening has been too sudden. . . . It's been impossible, as yet,
to look round. . . . This is the first moment that all the branches
of the tree have given way at the same moment. There is nothing
left to cling to, nothing on which one can get a hold. . . ."

There was something of desperation in the way he repeated
those words—"nothing, nothing at all. . . ." How deeply *was*
he committed?—on the edge of what abyss was he struggling?
Afraid that he might have given himself away, he checked his
flow of eloquence, fell back on the usual commonplaces—the
drive for industrial reequipment in the postwar period, over-
production, the fall in purchasing power. What he said did not
matter: it was this desperation of his that held my attention. It
was borne in on me at that moment that my hatred was dead,
and dead, too, my desire for reprisals. Perhaps they had been
dead for a long time. I had been piling coals on my anger,
had been tearing myself to pieces. But what was the use of
refusing to look facts in the face? My feelings, as I sat there in

my son's presence, were confused, but my dominant emotion was one of curiosity. How strange it all seemed—the wretched man's obvious agitation and terror, the horrors that it needed only a word from me to dissipate! I thought of the fortune that, so it seemed, had been my life's obsession. I had tried so hard to give it away or lose it. I had not been free even to dispose of it as I had wished, and now I felt, suddenly, wholly detached. It no longer interested me, was no longer any concern of mine. Hubert had left off speaking and was watching me from behind his spectacles. What was I scheming?—what new blow preparing? There was already a sort of fixed grin on his face. He drew himself up and raised his arm like a child preparing to ward off attack. He began again to speak, and now his voice was timid:

"All I ask is that you should set me on my feet. Taking into consideration what will be coming to me from Mamma, I shan't now need more than . . ." (he hesitated a moment before naming the figure) . . . "more than a million. Once I've wiped the slate clean, I shall be able to manage. Do what you like with the rest. . . . I undertake to bow to your wishes. . . ."

He swallowed and continued to observe me furtively. I was careful to keep my face a blank.

"And what about you, my dear?" I asked, turning to Geneviève. "You're right as rain, aren't you?—married to a clever husband. . . ."

It always irritated her to hear her husband praised. She protested that the business was on its last legs. Alfred had bought no rum, now, for two years. At least that meant that he had made no bad deals, which was a comfort. They'd got enough to live on, certainly, but Phili was threatening to desert his wife and child, and was waiting only until he knew for certain that all hope of getting some of the family fortune was gone. "Good riddance!" I muttered, but she took me up sharply.

"Oh, we all know he's a rotter—Janine no less than the rest of us—but if he leaves her she'll die. I mean it—she'll die. That's something you can't understand, Father: you're not made that way. Janine knows a great deal more about Phili than all the rest of us put together. She has often told me that he is far worse than we could possibly imagine. But that doesn't alter the fact that she would die if he left her. I know it must sound nonsense to you. Things like that are beyond your comprehension. But surely a man as intelligent as you can understand a thing even if you don't feel it?"

"You're tiring Papa, Geneviève. . . ." It had occurred to Hubert that his clumsy sister might have "put her foot in it," that I might be hurt in my pride by what she had said. He could see from my face that I was suffering, but he could not know why, could not know that Geneviève had opened an old wound and was jabbing at it.

"Lucky Phili!" I sighed.

I could read amazement in the glance that passed between my two children. They had always, quite honestly, believed me to be half-mad. Perhaps if they had had me locked up, they would have done so with an easy conscience.

"A blackguard!" muttered Hubert; "and he's got a hold over us!"

"His father-in-law looks on him with a rather kindlier eye," I said. "Alfred is always saying that he's a queer fish, but not really bad at heart."

Geneviève flared up:

"That's because he's got a hold over Alfred, too! The son-in-law has corrupted the father-in-law—everyone knows that! They're constantly being seen together consorting with women. . . . The shame of that was one of the things that made Mother's life a misery. . . ."

She dabbed at her eyes. It was clear that Hubert thought I was trying to distract their attention from what really mattered.

"That's not the point, Geneviève," he said with a show of irritation. "To hear you talk one would imagine that you and your children are the only people in the world."

She turned on him in a fury. Of the two of them, which was the most selfish?—that's what *she* would like to know!

"It's only natural," she went on, "to put one's own children first. I have always done everything for Janine, and I'm proud to admit it, just as Mamma did everything for us. I'd go through fire . . ."

Her brother broke in on her. I recognized myself in the sharpness of his tone. "And see that others went through it, too!" he said.

What fun I should once have got from their quarrel! I should have hailed with delight these preliminary signs of a battle to the death over the few leavings of my fortune, which I could not keep from them. But the only feeling of which I was conscious now was one of faint disgust and boredom. . . . If only the whole wretched business could be settled once and for all! If only they would leave me to die in peace!

"It's odd, my children," I said to them, "that I should end by doing what I've always considered as the height of folly. . . ."

Their snarlings were all forgotten in an instant! They turned on me a hard, suspicious look. They were waiting, their guard was up.

"I've always thought of myself in terms of the old farmer robbed of his livelihood and left by his children to die of hunger. If he took too long over his dying, well then, a few eiderdowns piled conveniently on his face would hasten the processes of nature. . . ."

"Father, *please* . . ."

The look of horror with which they protested was not assumed. Hastily I changed my tone.

"You're going to be busy, Hubert. Sharing out the pickings won't be easy. I've got my money stowed away in a great number of places—here, in Paris, abroad. Then there's the real estate, my various houses. . . ."

At each word their eyes grew rounder. They couldn't believe their ears. I saw Hubert's thin hands open and shut.

"I want everything to be settled before my death, at the same time as you wind up your mother's estate. I shall retain Calèse for my own use, both the house and the park (the cost of upkeep and repairs to fall on you). I don't want to hear another word about the vines. A monthly income—the amount of which remains to be settled—will be paid me by my lawyer. . . . Just hand me my wallet . . . yes, it's in the left-hand pocket of my coat."

Hubert gave it to me with a trembling hand. I took out an envelope.

"This will give you some idea of the total amount of my fortune . . . you had better take it to Arcam, the barrister. . . . No, on second thought, it would be better to ring him up and ask him to come round. I'll give it him myself and confirm my dispositions in your presence."

Hubert took the envelope and said with an air of acute anxiety:

"You're not laughing at us, are you?"

"Ring up the lawyer: you'll soon see whether I'm laughing. . . ."

"No," he said; "not today, it would be scarcely decent. . . . We ought to wait a week."

He passed one hand over his eyes. Clearly, he was feeling ashamed, was forcing himself to think of his mother. He turned the envelope over and over in his fingers.

"All right then, open it," I said; "open it and read what's inside. You have my authority to do so."

He went quickly across to the window and broke the seal. He fell on the letter like a starving man on food. Geneviève could restrain herself no longer, but got up, joined him, and peered greedily over his shoulder.

I looked at the brother and sister. There was nothing in the sight to cause me horror. A man of business threatened with ruin; a father and a mother who had suddenly come into the millions that they had thought lost to them forever. No, they caused me no sense of horror. But my own indifference astonished me. I was like a patient who comes round from an operation and says that he has felt nothing. I had torn out of myself something that I had always thought was deeply rooted in my being—and I felt nothing but relief, nothing but a sort of physical lightness! I was breathing more easily. What, after all, had I been doing for years but trying to get rid of this fortune, trying to load it on to somebody who was not a member of my family? But always I had been deceived in the object of my wishes. We do not know what we desire: we do not love those whom we think we love.

I heard Hubert say to his sister: "It's enormous, simply enormous—a vast fortune!" They exchanged a few words in low voices. Geneviève declared that they could not accept such a sacrifice, that they had no wish to strip me naked.

The words "sacrifice" and "strip" sounded strange in my ears. Hubert was insistent.

"You have been influenced by the emotion of the moment. You think you are more ill than you are. You're not seventy. People with your ailment live to a great old age. After a while you will regret what you have done. I will relieve you of all business worries, if you like, but you must enjoy in peace what belongs to you. We want only what is just. We have never asked for anything but justice. . . ."

I was overcome by a sense of weariness. They saw my eyes close. I told them that my mind was made up, that I would say no more on the subject except in the presence of a lawyer. They were already at the door. Without turning my head, I called them back.

"I forgot to tell you that a monthly allowance of fifteen hundred francs is to be paid to my son Robert. I have promised him that. Remind me of it when we draw up the agreement."

Hubert blushed. This particular arrow had taken him by surprise. But Geneviève read no malice into what I had said. Round-eyed, she made a rapid calculation:

"Eighteen thousand francs a year," she said. "Don't you think that's rather a lot?"

XVIII

The grass looks lighter than the sky. A thin vapor is rising from the soaked earth. The ruts, brimming with rain, reflect a muddy blue. I feel as interested in everything as I used to do when Calèse still belonged to me. Now, I am possessed of nothing, yet do not feel my poverty. The sound, at night, of rain upon the rotting vines makes me no less sad than when I was the owner of the threatened crop. What I thought of as love of my land was no more than the physical instinct of the peasant; for I come of a long peasant line and was born of those who, through the centuries, had scanned the sky with anxious looks. The money to be paid to me each month will accumulate at the lawyer's. I have never wanted for anything. All my life long I have been the prisoner of a passion that never really possessed me. Like a dog barking at the moon, I was held in thrall by a reflection. Fancy waking up at sixty-eight! Fancy being reborn at the very moment of my death! If only I may be granted just a few more years, a few months, a few weeks. . . .

239

The nurse has gone. I am feeling much better. Amélie and Ernest, who served Isa, are to stay on with me. They know how to give injections. Everything lies ready to my hand, the little bottles of morphine and of nitrite. The children are so busy that they scarcely ever leave town. They turn up here only when they want to know something about a valuation. . . . They get along without too much quarreling. They are so terrified of being "done down" that they have agreed, rather foolishly, to divide up all the complete sets of damask linen and glassware. They would cut a piece of tapestry in two rather than let any one of them have the benefit of it. They would prefer to see everything spoiled than get unequal shares. It is what they call having a "passion for justice." They have spent their lives giving high-sounding names to sordid instincts. . . . No, I ought to scratch that sentence out. For all I know, they may be prisoners, as I was, of a passion that does not really go deep.

What do they think of me? That I have been beaten, presumably, that I have been forced to surrender. They've "got me." All the same, each time they visit me they show respect and gratitude. But that doesn't prevent them from being in a constant state of amazement at my attitude. Hubert, in particular, keeps a watchful eye on me. He is suspicious. He is not quite sure that I have been disarmed. You can be quite easy in your mind, my poor boy. I was never really an object of terror even when I returned as a convalescent to Calèse, and now . . .

The elms along the roads and the poplars in the meadows stand massed together. Between their dark-hued trunks, the mist accumulates, and the smoke of bonfires and the breath of the huge earth when it has drunk deep. For we have waked to find the autumn all about us. The grapes still glittering from the recent storm will never recover what this rainy August stole. But for us, perhaps, it is never too late. I must never stop telling myself that it is never too late.

It was from no feeling of devotion that I went into Isa's room the day after I got back. What led me there was idleness, that complete lack of occupation that seizes me in the country. I never know whether I most enjoy or dislike it. I was tempted to push the half-open door, the first door on the left at the top of the stairs. The window was flung back; the wardrobe and the chest of drawers were empty. The servants had swept the place clean, and the sun, even in the farthest corners, had eaten up the last impalpable remains of a completed destiny. The September afternoon was buzzing with sleepy flies. The thick round tops of the lime trees looked like bruised fruit. The blue, deep at the zenith, showed pale behind the dozing hills. A burst of laughter came up to me from some girl I could not see. Sun bonnets were moving among the vines. The grape harvest had begun.

But the wonder of life had withdrawn from Isa's room. A pair of gloves and an umbrella lying on the floor of the wardrobe looked dead. I gazed at the old stone mantelpiece on the spandrel of which were carved a spade, a sickle, and a blade of corn. These old-fashioned hearths, in which whole trunks can burn, are masked in summer by large screens of painted canvas. This particular one had a picture of two oxen plowing. One day, when I was very young, I had slashed it with a penknife in a fit of temper. It was only leaning against the fireplace. I tried to adjust it properly, but it fell, revealing the black square of the grate, filled with ashes. Then I remembered what the children had told me about Isa's last day at Calèse: "She was burning papers: we thought there was a fire." . . . I realized how strongly she must have felt the approach of death. It is impossible, at one and the same time, to think of one's own death and that of another person. Obsessed by the certainty of my approaching end, I had, quite naturally, not felt worried by Isa's blood pressure. "It's nothing—just old age," our idiotic children had gone on saying. But she, when she had kindled this great fire, had known that her hour was at hand. She had wanted to disappear utterly and so had set about effacing every tiny trace of herself. I stared into the hearth, at the scraps of grey fluff that the wind was gently fluttering. The tongs she had used were still in their place, between the chimney and the wall. I took them and started to rummage in the heap of dust, that last remains of an utter nothingness.

I searched as though the secret of my life lay hidden there, the secret of our two lives. The farther I probed with the poker, the thicker lay the ashes. I brought out a few scraps of paper that the thickness of the bundles must have saved from the flame. But all I could recover were a few words, a few broken phrases, which conveyed no meaning. All were in the same handwriting. I could not recognize it. My hands were trembling: I worked feverishly. On one tiny fragment, smeared with soot, I could make out the word PAX. Beneath it was a small cross, a date, 23 February, 1913, and the words *"my dear daughter. . . ."* I set myself to assemble the letters written on the margin of some other pieces of charred paper, but all I could get was this: *"You are not responsible for the hatred that this rouses in you. Only if you yielded to it would you be to blame. Far from that being so, you try . . ."* As the result of much effort, I succeeded in reading a little more: *". . . judge the dead rashly . . . the affection that he feels for Luc does not prove"* . . . Soot hid all of the rest, except one single phrase: *"Forgive, not knowing what it is that you have to forgive. . . . Offer for him your . . ."*

There would be time enough later for me to think of what I had read. My only concern at the moment was to find more. I searched every nook and cranny of the hearth, crouching so awkwardly that I found it difficult to breathe. The discovery of a notebook bound in American cloth set my heart beating. It looked intact, but, on examining it, I found that none of the pages had escaped the fire. The only words I could decipher were on the inside of the cover, in Isa's hand: FLOWERS OF THE SPIRIT, and, underneath, *"My name is not the name of him who damns: I am called Jesus"* (Christ to Saint François de Sales).

There were several more quotations, but all of them illegible, I spent some time longer bending over the burned-out ashes, but in vain. I could find nothing more. I scrambled to my feet and looked at my black hands. In the mirror I could see my smeared forehead. Suddenly, as in the days of my youth, I was seized with a longing to go for a walk. Forgetful of my heart, I hurried downstairs, far too fast.

For the first time for weeks I made my way to the vines. Half stripped of their fruit, they were slipping back into their winter sleep. The landscape was light and limpid. It seemed to have become distended, like those blue-tinted bubbles that Marie used to blow from the end of a hollow straw. Already the ruts and the deep hoof-marks of oxen were hardening under the influence of sun and wind. I walked on, carrying within me the picture of an unknown Isa, of a woman racked by powerful passions that only God could master. The busy housewife had, all the while, been a wildly jealous sister. Luc had been to her an object of loathing. . . . How could a grown woman have brought herself to hate a little boy? . . . Was it the thought of her own children that had been at the bottom of that bitter resentment, the knowledge that I loved Luc so much more deeply than I ever loved them? But Marinette, too, she had detested. . . . It was *I* who had caused her all that suffering. Yes, it was true, I had had it in my power to torture her! What a mad dance it had been! Marinette was dead, Luc, too, and now Isa: and here I was, an old man, still on his feet, it was true, but standing at the very edge of that same grave that had swallowed the rest of them, and filled with a wild delight because at last I knew that I had not been an object of indifference to her, but had raised a storm to beat about her heart.

It was laughable. I actually laughed aloud, panting a little, leaning against one of the vine stakes, and looking at the pale sea of mist in which villages and village churches and poplar-lined roads lay drowned. The setting sun pierced through with difficulty to light that buried world. I could feel, I could see, I could touch my guilt. It was not only that my heart had become a nest of vipers, that it had been filled with hatred for my children, with a lust for vengeance and a grasping love of money. What was worse than that was that I had refused to look beyond the tangle of vile snakes. I had treasured their knotted hideousness as though it had been the central reality of my being—as though the beating of the life blood in my veins had been the pulse of all those swarming reptiles. Not content with knowing, through half a century, only of myself what was not truly me at all, I had carried the same ignorance into my dealing with others. The expression of squalid greed on the faces of my children had held me fascinated. Confronted by Robert, I had been able to see only his stupidity, because it was all I had wanted to see. I had never once realized that the superficial appearance of others was something I must break through, a barrier that I must cross, if I was ever to make contact with the real man, the real woman beyond and behind it. That was the discovery I ought to have made when I was thirty or forty. . . .

But now I am an old man. The movement of my heart is too sluggish. I am watching the last autumn of my life as it puts the vines to sleep and stupefies them with its fumes and sunlight. Those whom I *should* have loved are dead, and dead, too, those whom I *could* have loved. I have neither the time now, nor the strength, to embark upon a voyage of exploration with the object of finding the reality of others. Everything in me, even my voice, even my gestures, belongs to the monster whom I reared against the world, the monster to whom I gave my name.

Were those, in strict accuracy, the thoughts on which I brooded as I stood leaning against a vine stake at the far end of one of the planted rows, with my face turned toward the gleaming hill slopes of Yquem under the setting sun? One incident there was—and I must mention it here—that doubtless made them clearer in my mind. But it did not create them. They were there already on that evening, as I walked back to the house, my heart filled with the peace that lay upon the earth. The shadows were lengthening. The whole earth was wide open, awaiting the bounty of nature. In the distance the half-glimpsed hills were like bowed shoulders patiently hoping for the darkness and the mist to cover them so that they might stretch themselves, perhaps, lie down and fall into a human sleep.

I had expected to find Geneviève and Hubert at the house. They had promised to dine with me. For the first time in my life I was looking forward to their company, was thinking of it in a mood of pleasurable anticipation. I was impatient to show them my change of heart. Not one minute must I lose in getting to know them, in getting them to know me. Would there be time, before I died, to put my new discovery to the test? I longed to drive posthaste to the goal of my children's affection, to break through every obstacle that stood between them and me. At last I had cut through the knot of vipers. So quickly would I win their love that when the moment came for them to close my eyes, they would do so with tears.

They had not yet arrived. I sat on the bench close to the road, listening to the passing cars. The more they delayed, the more did I long for them to come. Several times I had a return of my old anger. What did they care about keeping me waiting! It didn't matter to them if I suffered on their account! They were doing it on purpose! . . . But I took a hold on myself. There might be reasons for their lateness of which I knew nothing, and it was unlikely that they would be those on which I habitually fed my resentment. The gong sounded for dinner. I went to the kitchen to tell Amélie that we must wait a little longer. Only on very rare occasions did I venture into her world of black rafters and pendent hams. I sat down in a wicker chair close to the fire. Amélie, her husband, and Cazau, the bailiff, were there. I had heard their loud laughter while I was still some way off. As I entered the room they all fell silent. An atmosphere of respect and terror enveloped me. I never talk to servants. It is not that I am a difficult or unreasonable master, but simply that, for me, they don't exist. I don't see them. But this evening I found their presence comforting. Because my children had not turned up, I should have liked to eat my dinner on the corner of the table that the cook used for chopping up the joints.

Cazau had made his escape. Ernest was putting on a white jacket, preparatory to serving at table. I tried to find something to say, but all in vain. I knew absolutely nothing about these two human beings who had been our devoted attendants for the past twenty years. At last, I remembered that, in the old days, their married daughter from Sauveterre de Guyenne had been in the habit of coming to see them, and that Isa had always refused to pay her for the rabbit she brought, on the ground that she had so many meals in our house. Without turning my head, I rather hurriedly asked:

"And how is your daughter, Amélie? Still living at Sauveterre?"

She bent her suntanned face to mine and stared.

"Surely, sir, you know that she is dead? . . . It'll be ten years on the twenty-ninth, Michaelmas Day . . . have you forgotten, sir?"

Her husband said nothing, but his eyes looked hard. He thought I had been only pretending to forget. I stammered out: "Oh, I'm so sorry! . . . this old head of mine . . ."—but, as always when I am embarrassed or nervous, I giggled. I just could not help it. Then the man announced in his usual voice that dinner was ready.

I got up at once, went into the ill-lit dining room, and sat down opposite the ghost of Isa. There, next to her, was where Geneviève has always sat, and then, in order, the Abbé Ardouin, Hubert. . . . My eyes wandered to Marie's high chair, standing between the sideboard and the window. It had descended, first to Janine, then to Janine's daughter. I went through the pretense of swallowing a few mouthfuls. . . . The expression on the face of the man who was serving me was horrible.

A fire of vine shoots had been lit in the drawing room. Here, each generation as it ebbed had left its shells—its albums, caskets, daguerreotypes, and patent lamps. The small tables were covered with knickknacks from which all life had drained away. The heavy tread of a horse in the night, the sound of the wine press that is built on to the house, tore at my heart strings. "Oh, my children, why didn't you come?" The words were the formulation of my wretchedness. Had the servants been listening outside the door, they would have thought there was a stranger in the room with me, for neither voice nor words would they have connected with the miserable old man, who, as they believed, had deliberately pretended not to know that their daughter was dead.

All of them, wife, children, masters, and servants, were in league against my soul. I must play my hateful part at their dictation. I was painfully caught in the rigidity of the expected attitude. I had modeled myself on the image projected by their hatred. What madness, at sixty-eight, to hope to swim against the stream, to impose on them a new vision of the person I really am and have always been! We see only what we are accustomed to see. You, too, my poor children, I do not truly see. Were I younger, the lines would be less deeply graven, the habits less unalterably rooted. But I doubt whether, even in my youth, I could have broken the spell. Some especial strength was needed, I said to myself. Yes, but what strength? The aid of some *person*, of someone in whom we might all have been reunited, of someone who would, in the eyes of my family, have guaranteed the victory that I had won over myself, of someone who would stand my witness, who might relieve me of my hideous burden, and bear it on his own shoulders. . . .

Even the genuinely good cannot, unaided, learn to love. To penetrate beyond the absurdities, the vices, and, above all, the stupidities of human creatures, one must possess the secret of a love that the world has now forgotten. Until that secret shall have been rediscovered, all betterment in conditions of life will be in vain. I used to think that it was selfishness that kept me uninterested in questions of sociology and economics, and to some extent that was true, for I have been a monster of solitude and indifference. Still, I had a feeling, an obscure certainty, that it was no use merely to revolutionize the face of the world, that what was needed was the power to reach the world through the medium of the heart. Him whom I seek can alone achieve that victory, and he must needs be the heart of all hearts, the burning center of all love. The desire I felt may well have been a prayer. On that night I was within an ace of falling on my knees with my arms on the back of a chair, as Isa used to do, long summers ago, with the three children pressing round her. In those days I would come back from the terrace toward the lighted window. I would muffle my footsteps and, invisible in the darkness of the garden, look on the group at prayer within. *"Prostrate at thy feet, O God"*—Isa would say—*"I thank thee that thou hast given me a heart to know and love thee. . . ."*

I remained standing in the middle of the room, swaying on my feet as though I had received a blow. I thought of my life and saw what it had been. No one could swim against such a current of mud. I had been a man so horrible that he could have no friend. But wasn't that, I asked myself, because I had always been incapable of wearing a disguise? If all men went through life with unmasked faces, as I had done for half a century, one might be surprised to find how little difference there was between them. But, in fact, no one lives with his face uncovered, no one. Most men ape greatness or nobility. Though they do not know it, they conform to certain fixed types, literary or other. This the saints know, and they hate and despise themselves because they see themselves with unclouded eyes. I should not have been so universally condemned had I not been so defenseless, so open, and so naked.

Such were the thoughts that haunted me that evening as I wandered about the darkened room, stumbling against those heavy pieces of furniture in mahogany and rosewood, poor wrecks buried in the sands of a family's past, on which so many bodies now turned to dust had at one time leaned and lain. Children's boots had soiled the sofa where they had snuggled with a volume of *Le Monde Illustré* of 1870. The dark stains on its covering were as they had always been. The wind was moaning round the house, stirring the dead leaves of the limes. In one of the rooms the shutters had been forgotten and left open.

XIX

Next day I waited impatiently for the coming of the postman. I paced up and down the garden as Isa used to do when the children were late and she felt anxious. Had they quarreled? Was one of them ill? I fretted myself "into a fever," and became as clever as Isa had ever been in the art of formulating and encouraging fixed ideas. I walked among the vines with the absentminded and remote look of those who brood upon a trouble. But I remember, too, that I noticed this change in myself and derived no little pleasure from the realization that I was ill at ease. The mist was a sounding board. I could hear the plain, though I could not see it. Wagtails and thrushes were making merry in the furrows where the grapes were not yet rotting. Luc, as a child, when the holidays were ending, had loved these sober-footed mornings. . . .

A line from Hubert, dated Paris, did little to reassure me. He had been obliged, he said, to leave in a hurry. Something serious had happened. He would tell me about it on his return, which would be, he hoped, in two days' time. My mind immediately went to difficulties of a financial nature. Had he, perhaps, been doing something illegal?

By the afternoon I could stand the suspense no longer. I had myself driven to the station, where I took a ticket to Bordeaux, though I had promised not to do any more traveling alone. Geneviève was now living in our old house. I ran into her in the hall, just as she was saying good-bye to someone I did not know, but who looked like a doctor.

"Hasn't Hubert told you?"

She took me into the waiting room where I had fainted on the day of the funeral. I breathed more freely when I knew what the trouble was. Phili had run away. I had feared something much worse. But he had gone in company with a woman who had "a hold on him," and after a terrible scene that had left Janine without a vestige of hope. The poor child was in a state of complete prostration from which it seemed impossible to rouse her, and the doctor was worried. Alfred and Hubert had pursued the fugitive to Paris. Judging from a telegram that had just arrived, their efforts had been fruitless.

"When I think of the allowance we made them . . . Of course we were wise to possible risks and had not given them control of any capital. Still, the income was by no means inconsiderable. Janine was always terribly weak with him. He could get anything he wanted out of her and was constantly threatening to abandon her, because he felt convinced that you were not going to leave us anything. It's so extraordinary to me that he should have chosen just the very moment when you'd handed over the whole of your fortune to run away—how do you explain it?"

She came to a dead stop, her eyebrows raised, her eyes dilated. Then she leaned against the radiator, rubbing her hands together.

"This woman," I said, "is, I suppose, rich?"

"Far from it—she's a teacher of singing. You know her quite well: it's Madame Vélard. She's by no means young, and she's knocked about a bit. It's all she can do to make a living. How do you explain it?" she said again.

She did not wait for my answer, but went on talking. At that moment Janine came into the room. She was wearing a dressing gown, and put up her face for me to kiss. She was no thinner, but despair had wiped the heavy, unattractive face clean of all that, at one time, I had hated in it. The poor creature, formerly so daubed and mannered, had become frighteningly simple and bare. The crude light of a hanging lamp beat down on her, but she stood there unblinking. All she said was, "I suppose you know," and collapsed onto the sofa.

I don't think she even heard what her mother was saying, the interminable catalogue of grievances that Geneviève must have been pouring out over and over again since Phili left.

"When I think . . ."

Every sentence began with that "When I think . . ."—a surprising statement from one who thought so little. They had, she said, consented to the marriage, although, at twenty-two, Phili had already run through a considerable fortune that had come to him while he was still very young (in view of the fact that he was an orphan and had no near relations, it had seemed best to give him full control of his money). The family had shut their eyes to the very unsavory life he had been leading . . . and this was all the thanks they got! . . .

I tried in vain to control my mounting irritation. My old perversity stirred in its sleep. As though Geneviève herself, Alfred, Isa, and all their friends, had not been continually at Phili, holding out a thousand dazzling prospects!

"What I find quite extraordinary," I said, "is that you seem really to believe what you're saying. And yet, you must know that you were all of you running after him. . . ."

"I won't have you stick up for him, Father! . . ."

I protested that it was not a question of sticking up for him. But we had been wrong to paint Phili blacker than he was. No doubt he had been made to see too clearly that, once the fortune was assured, he would have to swallow every kind of insult, that they were banking on his becoming resigned to having his wings clipped. The trouble was that human beings are never so base as we believe them to be.

"When I think that you can stand there and defend a wretched creature who has abandoned his young wife and his little girl . . ."

"Geneviève!" I cried in exasperation. "You don't begin to understand what I am saying. Do at least make an effort. I quite agree that it is a shocking thing for a man to abandon his wife and child, but the culprit might have yielded to ignoble motives instead of to higher ones. . . ."

"So you think it noble," said Geneviève, with mulish obstinacy, "to abandon a wife of twenty-two and a young child. . . ."

That was the limit of her vision. She simply had no idea of what I was talking about.

"Oh, don't be such a fool . . . unless it is that you are deliberately pretending not to understand. My point is that I find Phili a good deal less despicable now that . . ."

Geneviève cut me short, saying that I might at least wait until Janine had left the room before insulting her with this defense of her husband. But the girl who, until now, had not opened her lips, suddenly said, in a voice that I had difficulty in recognizing:

"What's the use of denying it, Mamma? We treated Phili like mud. Don't pretend you've forgotten. When all this business of sharing out Grand'pa's money began, we thought we'd got him where we wanted him. He was just like a dog I was dragging about on a lead. I had resigned myself to the fact that he didn't love me. That didn't hurt anymore. I had got him: he was mine; he belonged to me. I held the purse strings and I could make him pay through the nose. That was your expression, Mamma. Don't you remember how you said to me: 'Now you can make him pay through the nose . . .'? We thought that money was the only thing he cared about. He may have thought so, too, but his anger and his sense of humiliation were too much for him. Because, you see, he doesn't love this woman who's stolen him away. He told me so himself, before he left, and he flung so many horrible things in my face that I am sure he was speaking the truth. The point is that she doesn't despise him and doesn't make him feel like a worm. She gave herself to him: she didn't snatch him. I was just handed to him on a plate!"

She repeated the last words as though she were flagellating herself. Her mother shrugged, but was pleased to see her tears. . . . "She'll feel better after this." Then she went on: "Don't worry, darling, he'll come back. Hunger drives the wolf out of the woods. . . . When he's been roughing it for a bit . . ."

I felt sure that talk like that would only disgust Janine. I got up and took my hat. The idea of spending the rest of the evening with my daughter was more than I could stand. I told her that I had hired a car and was going back to Calèse. Suddenly Janine said:

"Take me with you, Grand'pa. . . ."

Her mother asked her whether she had gone mad. She must stay where she was. The lawyers needed her presence. Besides, she would be "miserable" at Calèse.

She followed me out on to the landing and attacked me violently for having humored Janine.

"You must admit that if she gets rid of that creature it'll be a case of good riddance. One can always get an annulment, and with all that money Janine might make a splendid marriage. But she's got to be quit of him first. . . . You always detested Phili, and now you must needs go singing his praises to her. . . . Whatever happens, she mustn't go to Calèse . . . a nice state she'd come back in! Sooner or later, if she stays here, we shall manage to take her mind off her troubles . . . she'll forget. . . ."

Unless she dies, I thought, or drags on a miserable existence with a pain that never lessens, that no lapse of time will ever change. It may be that Janine belongs to that peculiar race of human beings that an old lawyer is best fitted to understand. She may well be one of those women in whom hope is a disease, who can never be cured of hoping, and, at the end of twenty years, still watches the door with the eyes of a faithful dog. I went back into the room where Janine was still seated and said to her:

"When you're ready, my child. . . . You are always a welcome visitor."

She gave no sign that she had taken my meaning, Geneviève had followed me in, and now said, suspiciously: "What was that you were saying to her?" I learned later that she had accused me of having "changed Janine's mind" during the few seconds I was alone with her, of having "filled her head with all sorts of ideas." I went down the stairs, remembering only that the girl had said "take me with you. . . ." She had asked me to take her. Instinctively, I had, when talking of Phili, said just what she needed to hear. Maybe I was the first person who had not wounded her susceptibilities.

I walked through Bordeaux. It was the first day of the new term, and the streets were all aglitter. The mist had left a dampness on the pavements of the Cours de l'Intendance, and they shone. The voices of the noonday crowd drowned the rattle of the trams. I was no longer aware of the smells of my childhood. I might have found them again in the melancholy surroundings of the Rue Dufour-Dubergier, of the Rue de la Grosse Cloche. There, perhaps, I might have come, at some dark street corner, on an old woman hugging a steaming pot of those boiled chestnuts that smell of aniseed. I did not feel sad. Someone had listened to me and had understood.

The two of us had come together, and that, in itself, spelled victory. But with Geneviève I had failed. When I am faced by a certain type of idiocy I can do nothing. One can touch a living soul through a curtain of vice and crime no matter how dense and dark: but vulgarity is an insurmountable barrier. Well, it couldn't be helped. I would follow my own line. Impossible to shatter the stones of all these graves. It would mean happiness for me if I could reach to the heart of one single being before I died.

I slept at a hotel and did not return to Calèse until the following morning. A few days later Alfred came to see me, and from him I learned that my visit had had disastrous results. Janine had written Phili a crazy letter in which she said that she had been to blame for everything, and had asked him to forgive her. "Women are all the same. . . ." I knew what the fat idiot was thinking, though he did not dare to put it into words: "She's her grandmother all over again."

He made it quite clear that a suit for separation would now stand no chance of success and that Geneviève held me responsible. I had worked on Janine. I asked my son-in-law with a smile what possible motives I could have had for doing a thing like that. He didn't, he said, share his wife's point of view, but explained that, according to her, I had acted from malice, from a desire to revenge myself, perhaps even from sheer love of mischief.

The children did not come to see me again. Two weeks later, Geneviève wrote me a letter in which she explained that they had had to send Janine to a nursing home. There was no question, of course, of insanity. They had great hopes that, if she were left to herself, she would get better.

I, too, was left to myself. I felt perfectly well. Never had I had so long a respite from my heart. For the whole of that fortnight, and well beyond it, the autumn sunshine lay upon the earth, as though reluctant to depart. Not a leaf had fallen yet, and the roses bloomed again. This new estrangement from my children should have made me suffer. Hubert put in an appearance only when there was business to discuss. He was dry and formal, perfectly polite, but on his guard. The influence that, my children insisted, I had brought to bear on Janine had lost me all the ground that I had gained. In their eyes I was once more the enemy, a treacherous old man, capable of anything. The only one of them all who might have understood me was shut away and cut off from all communication with the living. But I was conscious only of a deep sense of peace. Stripped of everything, isolated, and with a terrible death hanging over my head, I remained calm, watchful, and mentally alert. The thought of my melancholy existence did not depress me, nor did I feel the burden of my empty years. . . . It was as though I were not a sick old man, as though I still had a lifetime before me, as though the peace of which I was possessed was Somebody.

XX

It is a month now since Janine ran away from the nursing home and came here. She is not yet cured. She believes that she has been the victim of a plot and says that she was shut away because she refused to attack Phili and ask him for a separation and an annulment. The others imagine that it is I alone who have put these ideas into her head and have set her against them, whereas, if the truth be told, I have been fighting tooth and nail, all through the interminable days at Calèse, against her illusions and her fancies.

Outside, the rain has been rotting the leaves and making them indistinguishable from the mud. Heavy clogs crunch the gravel of the courtyard. A man passes, his head enveloped in a sack. So stripped has the garden become that there is nothing left to disguise the few poor concessions made to pleasure—mere skeletons of hedgerows, sparse shrubberies shivering under the eternal rain. So penetrating is the dampness of the rooms that, when night comes, we lack the courage to move far from the drawing room fire. Midnight sounds, but we cannot bring ourselves to go to bed. The embers, patiently piled, collapse in ashes, and I have to renew the old wearisome effort to convince the poor girl that her parents, her brother, and her uncle have no malevolent designs on her. I do my best to keep her mind from dwelling on the nursing home. The conversation always, in the end, comes back to Phili: "You've no idea what he was really like, the kind of man he was at bottom. . . ." I can never feel sure whether these phrases are a prelude to a list of grievances or to a lyrical outburst. Only the tone in which they are spoken gives me a clue, makes it possible for me to know whether she is about to sing his praises or bespatter him with mud. In either case, the facts that she produces seem to me to be equally insignificant. The poor creature is entirely without imagination, but love has given her an extraordinary power of distortion and amplification. I know her Phili only too well. He is one of those completely negative human beings whom youth, for one fleeting moment, manages to invest with glamour. To this spoiled child, born with a silver spoon in his mouth, she attributes subtleties of feeling, capabilities of villainy and premeditated treacheries—though, as a matter of fact, he is nothing but a mass of automatic reflexes.

What she won't understand is that what he really needs is to feel that he is strong. It was no use trying to bully him. Dogs of his type don't respond to that kind of treatment. They merely slink away and pick up what they can find lying to hand.

She hasn't got the remotest idea of what he is really like. All she knows is that she longs to have him with her. All she feels is a hunger for the endearments that he withholds and bitter jealousy and horror at the thought that she has lost him. Without eyes to see, a nose to smell, nerves to feel, she runs after him in a demented way, without having the faintest idea of what it is she is pursuing. . . . Are fathers ever really blind? Janine is my granddaughter, but were she my daughter I should still see her for what she is—one of those women who are incapable of receiving anything from another person. With her regular features, her thick, heavy body, and her foolish voice, she is marked with the sign of those who never catch the eye or fill the mind. Nevertheless, when I sit talking to her at night, I find a sort of beauty in her, a beauty not her own but borrowed from despair. Surely there must be a man somewhere whom this display of heat and flame might attract? At present she is burning away unhappily in a wasteland beneath a darkened sky, with nobody to see her but an old crock.

Though I have come to pity her in the course of our long vigils, I never tire of making comparison between Phili, who is as like a million others as one white butterfly is like all other white butterflies, and this frenzy of passion that he alone can rouse in his wife, so that nothing else in the whole world, visible or invisible, exists for her. Janine can, quite literally, see nothing but this slightly shop-soiled male who prefers drink to most other forms of self-indulgence, and looks on love as a labor, a duty, and a bore. . . . What a tragedy it is!

Sometimes her daughter slips into the room, but she scarcely looks at her, just kisses her curly head in a mechanical sort of way. Not that the child is wholly without influence on her. It was because of her that Janine screwed herself to the point of abandoning her pursuit of Phili (she is quite capable of hounding him, goading him, and making scenes in public). *I* couldn't have stopped her. It is for the child's sake that she has stayed on here. But motherhood has brought her no consolation. It was in my arms, on my knees, that the little girl sought refuge one night as we sat waiting for dinner to be announced. There was a birdlike, nestlike fragrance in her hair that brought back memories of Marie. I closed my eyes and pressed my lips to her head. I restrained myself from hugging her too tightly, while, in my heart, I called upon my long-dead child. It was Luc, too, whom I felt I was embracing. When she was hot from play she had the same salty taste that I used to find in his cheeks when, tired out from running, he fell asleep at table. On those occasions he could not even wait for the dessert, but would go round the company holding up his drowsy face for good-night kisses. . . .

So it was that I dreamed, while Janine moved about the room, pacing, pacing, within the prison of her love.

I remember another evening when she asked: "What can I do to get rid of this pain? . . . Do you think it will ever go away?" There was a frost. I watched her open the window and push back the shutters. She bathed her face, her breast, in the frozen radiance of the moon. I led her back to the fire and, though I am inexpert in the gestures of love, sat awkwardly beside her with my arm about her shoulders. Was there nothing, I asked, that could bring her comfort? "You have your faith." "Faith?" she said vaguely, as though she had not understood. "Yes," I went on, "God. . . ." She raised her ravaged face, and her eyes were full of suspicion. At last she said that she "couldn't see the connection," but I was insistent, and she continued:

"I'm religious, if that is what you mean. I go to church. Why do you ask me a question like that? Are you laughing at me?"

"Are you quite certain," I went on, "that Phili is really worth all this pain and torment?"

She looked at me with the same morose, irritated expression that I am used to seeing on Geneviève's face when she doesn't understand what has been said to her, doesn't know what answer to make, and fears a trap. Finally, she plucked up courage to say that the two things "had nothing to do with one another" . . . that she didn't like mixing up religion with matters of this kind, that she was a practicing Christian and regularly performed her religious duties, but that she had a horror of morbidity. She might have been saying that she always paid her taxes. It is precisely the attitude that, all my life, I have loathed and detested, the caricature and mean interpretation of the Christian life that I had deliberately chosen to regard as the essence of the religious mind, in order that I might feel free to hate it. One must have the courage to look what one hates full in the face. . . . But had I not already been guilty of self-deception, I asked myself, when, on the terrace at Calèse, the Abbé Ardouin had said: "You are a very good man"? Later, I had shut my ears so as not to hear Marie's words as she lay dying. Nevertheless, at her bedside the secret of death and of life had been revealed to me. . . . A little girl had been dying for me . . . that was something that I had tried to forget. With untiring assiduity I have always tried to find some way of losing the key that a mysterious hand has invariably given to me at the great turning points of my life (the expression of Luc's face after Mass on Sunday mornings when the grasshoppers were beginning to scrape, and again this spring, on the night of the hailstorm . . .).

So ran my thoughts that evening. I remember getting up and pushing back my chair so violently that Janine gave a start. The silence of Calèse at that late hour, a thick, an almost solid silence, numbed and muted her grief. She let the fire die down, and, as the room grew colder, moved her chair closer to the hearth until her feet were almost touching the embers. The dying flames seemed to exert a kind of attraction on her hands and face. The lamp on the chimney piece shone down on her heavy, crouching figure, while I wandered about among the mahogany and rosewood in the encumbered dark. Impotently I prowled around that lump of humanity, that bruised and beaten body. "My child . . . ," I began, but could find no words for what I wanted to say. . . . Something, as I sit tonight writing these lines, is stifling me, something is making my heart feel as though it would burst—it is the Love whose name at last I know, whose ador . . .

❋

Calèse, 10 December 193—

My dear Geneviève:

The drawers here are positively bursting with papers, but I hope, by the end of this week, to have got them into some sort of order. My immediate duty, however, is to send on to you at once the strangest of strange documents. You know that our father died at his desk, and that Amélie found him on the morning of November 24 with his face fallen forward on an open notebook. It is this book that is now on its way to you by registered post.

I am afraid that you will be as pained as I was when you read it. . . . Fortunately, the writing is so bad that the servants will make nothing of it. At first, from motives of delicacy, I decided to keep it from you, thereby saving you a good deal of distress, for it contains passages in which father speaks of you in a way that cannot but wound your susceptibilities. But then I wondered whether I had any right to keep to myself something that is yours as much as mine. You know how scrupulous I am in all that pertains to our parents, and I feel sure that you will understand what prompted me to change my mind. None of us, if it comes to that, shows up very well in these embittered pages. They tell us—alas!—nothing that we have not long known. The contempt with which father treated me poisoned my early years. For a considerable period of my life I had no confidence in myself. I quailed beneath that pitiless eye, and it was a long time before I even began to realize my true worth.

I have forgiven him, however, and perhaps I ought to add that what now urges me to bring this document to your notice is, for the most part, a sense of filial duty. Judge him how we may, there can be no doubt that our father emerges from these pages—in spite of the horrible things he says—I won't say as more noble, but certainly as more human (I am thinking, in particular, of his love for our sister Marie, and for young Luc—of which there is much moving evidence). I am in a far better position now to understand the grief that he displayed when our mother died, grief that, at the time, came to us as a staggering surprise. You thought it, I remember, to some extent put on. Should what is there written do no more than throw a light on the feelings that lay so deeply buried beneath the surface of his relentless pride, your reading of his confession will amply compensate for the pain it must otherwise, my dear Geneviève, cause you.

I am grateful for it—as I think you too will be—if only because it serves to ease our conscience. I am by nature a worrier. No matter how many reasons I may have for feeling that I am in the right, a very little will start me on a long process of self-examination. For one who has developed moral sensibility, as I have done, to a high degree, life can never be easy. Pursued by a father's hatred, I have never had recourse to even the most legitimate methods of defense without being oppressed by feelings of anxiety—I would even say, of remorse. Had it not been that I was the head of the family, and, as such, responsible for the honor of our name and the well-being of our children, I should often have been tempted to give up the struggle rather than suffer those torments and strugglings of the spirit of which you have, more than once, been a witness.

I thank God who, in his mercy, has seen fit to justify me through these, our father's, written words. In the first place, they provide confirmation of what we had long suspected about his various schemes for depriving us of our birthright.

It is not without a sense of shame that I read about the ways in which he hoped to establish a hold over both Bourru the lawyer and that young chap Robert. Over these disgraceful incidents it is well that we should cast the mantle of Noah. Still, the fact remains that it was my bounden duty to frustrate, at any cost, his many abominable machinations. This I did, and with a success of which I see no reason to be ashamed. Of one thing, my dear sister, you may rest assured: that you owe your fortune to *me*. In what he has written, the wretched man tried hard to convince himself that the hatred that he felt for us died a sudden death. He takes pride in announcing that all concern for worldly goods left him in a flash. I must confess that when I read that I found it very difficult not to laugh! But it is worth noticing the precise moment of this unexpected change of front. It occurred just when his schemes had gone awry, when his natural son had agreed, for a price, to tell us what he knew of them. It was not easy for him to get rid of so huge a fortune. Plans that it had taken him years to perfect could not be rearranged in a few days. The truth of the matter is that the poor man felt his end to be near and had neither the time nor the means to disinherit us except in the manner that he had decided to adopt, and that we providentially discovered.

As a lawyer he was unwilling to lose his case in the court either of his own or of our judgment. Consequently, he was cunning enough—though half-unconsciously, I admit—to transform actual defeat into moral victory. He persuaded himself that he was no longer interested, that he had become detached from the things of this world. . . . What else could he have done? I, certainly, am not prepared to have dust thrown in my eyes, and I feel pretty sure that you have enough good sense to agree. We need not, I think, go out of our way to admire or to be grateful.

There is another point of which this narrative lifts a weight from my conscience. It is something about which I have long indulged in heart searchings, though *I* have never succeeded, I must admit, in altogether ridding myself of a pricking sense of guilt. I refer to the efforts we made—though they came to nothing—to get the view of a specialist on the subject of father's mental condition. I ought, I think, to make it clear that much of my uneasiness on this score sprang from the attitude taken by my wife. I never, as you know, attach very much importance to her opinion. No one could well be less capable than she of holding balanced views on any subject. But in this matter of the specialist she gave me no rest, night or day, and was forever dinning into my ears arguments, some of which, I now admit, did go home and did make me feel uncomfortable. She succeeded at last in convincing me that father, who had been a great chancery barrister, a shrewd man of business, and a profound student of psychology, must be good-sense incarnate. . . . Nothing is easier than to paint an ugly picture of children who try to get their old father certified so as not to lose their inheritance . . . you see, I am not mincing words . . . and I have, God knows, spent many a sleepless night brooding on the problem.

Well, my dear Geneviève, this notebook, especially in its final pages, provides ample evidence that the poor man was suffering from intermittent delirium. I am prepared to go further, and to say that we should have been fully justified in submitting the case to a psychiatrist. But what is now far more important is that pages containing so much that might prove dangerous to our children must on no account be divulged to any living soul. I may as well say, at once, that I consider it to be your duty to burn what I have sent as soon as you have read it to the end. We *must not* run the risk of it falling under the eyes of a stranger. You cannot but realize, my dear Geneviève, that though *we* have always maintained the strictest secrecy about our family affairs, that though I have always taken steps to see that nothing should leak out concerning the uneasiness we have all felt about the mental state of him who, when all's said and done, was the head of the clan, others, not strictly members of it, have been far from showing the same discretion, or even common prudence. Your wretched son-in-law, especially, has been guilty of spreading the most dangerous stories. We are paying a high price for them now, and I am sure that I am not telling you anything that you don't know already when I say it is common talk in Bordeaux that there is a close connection between Janine's neurasthenia and the eccentricities popularly attributed to your father as a result of Phili's gossiping.

Tear the thing up, then, and don't talk of it to a soul. I would go further and say—let there be no mention of it even among ourselves. I don't mind admitting that this extreme caution may, in some ways, be a matter for regret. There are in our father's narrative certain psychological observations, certain impressions of nature, that show that his oratorical training had left him with a real gift for writing. That is but one reason the more for destroying it. A nice thing it would be, wouldn't it, if, at some later date, one of the children should think of publishing it?

But there can be no reason why you and I should not call things by their proper names. Now that we have read this record through, we can have few illusions about father's semi-insanity. I can see now what your daughter meant (at the time I took it for a sick woman's whim) when she said: "Grand'pa is the only truly religious person I have ever met." The poor child had let herself be taken in by his vague aspirations and hypochondriacal fancies. All through his life he had been the enemy of his family, hated by everybody, and without a single friend. He had been unfortunate in love, as you will see (there are some very comic details in this connection!), and so jealous of his wife that he could never forgive her for having indulged in a harmless flirtation when she was a girl. Is it conceivable that, toward the end of his life, he should have felt a desire for the consolations of prayer? I don't think so. What emerges from these pages with dazzling clarity is a state of well-defined mental instability, taking the form of persecution mania and religious hallucination. Is there no trace, you will ask, of genuine Christianity? None at all. Anyone as deeply informed as I am about such matters knows only too well the real value of such outbursts. Not to put too fine a point on it, bogus mysticism of this kind makes me feel physically sick.

But you, being a woman, may feel differently. Should you be inclined, then, to take his religiosity at its face value, all I can say is this: remember that father, with his extraordinary gift for hatred, never loved anything unless it provided him with a *weapon against somebody*. This religious exhibitionism of his amounts only to a criticism, direct or oblique, of the principles in which our mother brought us up from childhood. If he indulged in a murky mysticism, it was only that he might use it as a stick to beat that rational and moderate faith that has always held a place of honor in our family. Truth is poise . . . but I will not plunge deeper into those regions of abstract thought where you would have difficulty in following me. I have said enough. Read the document for yourself. I am impatient to know what you make of it.

I have little space left in which to reply to the important matters on which you have asked my opinion. My dear Geneviève, we are living in days of crisis, and the problems with which we are faced are agonizing. If we keep these piles of banknotes tucked away in a safe, we shall have to live on capital—and that is always a misfortune. If, on the contrary, we instruct our broker to buy shares, the dividends we may get will be small consolation for the continual fall in the capital value of our investments. Since whatever we do we are bound to lose, the wiser course will be to keep our Bank of France notes. The franc is worth only four sous, but it is backed by an immense gold reserve. On this point father was clear sighted, and we ought to follow his example. There is one temptation, my dear Geneviève, against which you must fight tooth and nail—the temptation to invest at any price. It is deeply rooted in the French temperament. We shall, of course, have to watch every penny we spend. Should you ever want any advice, you know that I am only too ready to give it. Times are bad, but profitable opportunities may occasionally present themselves. I am, at the moment, keeping a very close eye on a cinema concern and a new liqueur. Those are the type of investment that the crisis will not touch. In my opinion, it is things of that kind that we ought to watch. We must be bold, but, at the same time, prudent.

I am delighted to know that you have better news of Janine. I don't think that her excessive religious devotion, which makes you uneasy, need be considered as a serious danger. The important thing is that she should stop thinking about Phili. Her natural sense of proportion will reassert itself. She belongs to a race that has always known how not to misuse the *really good things*.

Until Tuesday, my dear Geneviève, HUBERT.

Janine to Hubert

My dear Uncle:

I am writing to ask whether you will act as judge between Mamma and me. She won't let me read Grand'pa's journal because she says it would damage the devotion I have to his memory. But if she's so keen that it shouldn't be damaged, why does she keep on saying: "You've no idea what awful things he says about you. He doesn't even spare your looks . . ."? I am even more surprised that she should be so eager for me to see the very harsh letter in which you expressed your views about the journal. . . .

Now, for the sake of peace and quiet, she says she'll let me have it if you think I may, and that she leaves the decision entirely to you. I am making this appeal, therefore, to your sense of justice.

Let me dispose at once of the first objection. It concerns me, and me alone. No matter how hard Grand'pa may be on me, he can't be harder than I am on myself, and I am quite sure that the sharp edge of his criticism spares the unhappy girl who spent one whole autumn with him in the house at Calèse, up to the time of his death.

Forgive me, Uncle, if I contradict you on one essential point. I am the only witness in a position to pronounce on the state of Grand'pa's feelings during those last weeks of his life. You denounce what you call his vague and morbid religiosity. But let me tell you this: he had three interviews (one at the end of October and two in November) with the curé of Calèse, whose evidence, for some reason that I can't fathom, you refuse to accept. According to Mother, the journal, in which he set down the most trivial incidents of his life, says nothing about those interviews, which wouldn't be the case if they had really been the occasion of a change in himself. . . . But she says, too, that it breaks off in the middle of a word. I have no doubt at all that death surprised your father at the very moment when he was about to make his declaration of faith. It's no use your saying that if he had received absolution he would have taken communion. I can only repeat what he told me the day before he died, that he was weighed down by a sense of unworthiness. The poor man had made up his mind to wait until Christmas. What reason have you for not believing me? Why treat me as though I were the victim of a hallucination? His voice is fresh in my memory. I can hear it now as it was when he spoke to me on the Wednesday, which was the day before his death, in the drawing room at Calèse. He said how eagerly he was looking forward to Christmas. It sounded as though he was in a condition of great mental suffering. Maybe the shadow of death was already upon him.

Don't be afraid, Uncle. I am not trying to make him out a saint. I agree with you that he was a terrible, even at times a dreadful, man. That doesn't alter the fact that a great light shone upon him during those last days of his life, and that it was he, and he alone, who, at that moment, took my face between his hands and entirely changed my way of looking at things. . . .

Doesn't it occur to you that your father might have been quite a different man if only *we* had been different? Don't accuse me of throwing stones at you. I know your good qualities, and I know that Grand'pa was cruelly unjust both to you and to Mother. The real misfortune for all of us was that he took us for exemplary Christians. . . . Don't protest. Since he died I have seen much of people who, in spite of all their faults and weaknesses, live according to their faith and move about their daily tasks in the fullness of grace. If Grand'pa had lived among them, mightn't he have discovered years ago the harbor that he reached at last only on the very threshold of death?

Let me say again that it is not my intention to abuse my family in the interest of its implacable head. I don't forget (far from it) that poor Grand'ma's example might, in itself, have been enough to open his eyes, had he not preferred to glut his feelings of resentment. But I do want you to know why, in the last resort, I feel that he was right in his attitude toward us. Where our treasure was, there were our hearts also. We thought of nothing but the threat to our inheritance. No doubt there was ample excuse for us. You were a businessman, I was a poor weak woman. But that doesn't alter the fact that, with the single exception of Grand'ma, we never let our principles interfere with our lives. Our thoughts, our desires, our actions struck no root in the faith to which we paid lip service. All our strength was employed in keeping our eyes fixed on material things, while Grand'pa . . . I wonder whether you will understand what I mean when I say that where his treasure was, there his heart was *not?* I am quite sure that on this point the document that you won't let me read contains conclusive evidence.

I do hope, Uncle, that you will see what I mean, and I await your reply with confidence.

JANINE.

Questions for Reflection and Discussion

Use the following questions as guides to deeper individual understanding of the novel or for group discussion.

1. How does the quote from St. Teresa of Ávila at the beginning of the book relate to the rest of the novel?

2. What is the "knot of vipers" in this novel? Is it more than one thing?

3. Describe the character of Louis before his change of heart. (p. 247) What motivated his choices during these years?

4. What was Louis's attitude toward organized religion during most of his life? How did his family's behavior reinforce his attitude? Did his family's behavior ever contradict his ideas? If so, how?

5. Why did Louis react as he did to Isa's youthful confession? Do you think his reaction was reasonable? Why or why not?

6. How was Louis's relationship to Marie different from the relationships he had with his other children? How did her death affect him? How did he experience her influence near the end of his life?

7. Why did Abbé Ardouin say that Louis was "a very good man?" (p. 106)

8. Does Louis or his family bear the greater responsibility for the destructive nature of their domestic life?

9. What impact did meeting Robert have on Louis?

10. What do you think caused the change in Louis's attitude toward his family and his fortune?

11. How did Louis's family react to his change?

12. What did Louis say about the consequences of his past choices? What impact had they had on him? What had he lost?

13. What was Louis trying to do at the end of his life that he felt he had never really done before? (p. 252)

14. Working from this novel, what is grace? How do we close ourselves off from grace? What is the price we pay? What happens when we open ourselves to God's grace?

15. What warnings does this novel offer you in the context of your own life? What hope does it offer?

About the Author

François Mauriac was born in 1885 in Bordeaux, France. His father died when Mauriac was two years old, and he, his four siblings, and his mother then moved in with grandparents. As a child, Mauriac was educated by the Marianite religious order, and as a young man at the University of Bordeaux. In 1908, Mauriac was accepted for graduate studies in Paris, but left after a few months to devote his life to literature.

His first published work was a book of poetry. After World War I, during which he served as a hospital orderly in the Balkans, Mauriac published his first novels, of which *The Kiss of the Leper* (1922) gained the most renown, as well as criticism from some Catholics.

Mauriac's childhood religious formation had been strongly Jansenistic. Jansenism was a heresy with a particular hold in France that, despite being condemned by the church several times in the seventeenth and eighteenth centuries, remained a strong presence in popular French piety. Jansenism denied humanity's free will and was noted for its moral strictness and emphasis on religious observance.

Mauriac's work reflects this formation in its frequent darkness, emphasis on sin, continual fundamental struggle between nature and grace, and sometimes critical or even satirical portrayals of the hypocrisies of the French Catholic middle class.

It is this last point that riled critics of *The Kiss of the Leper*, the story of a young woman's life ruined by her family, as they sought to control who she would marry.

In subsequent novels, Mauriac took up the theme and deepened his portrayals of individuals rooted in sin, obsession, and repression, and the grace available to them at their fingertips, sometimes, paradoxically, because of their sin. *The Desert of Love* (1925) and *Thérèse Desqueyroux* (1927) are two notable works from this period. Two of Mauriac's finest novels from later years are *Vipers' Tangle* (1932) and *A Woman of the Pharisees* (1941).

Mauriac's pen produced more than fiction. He was a prolific writer of all genres, including poetry, drama, literary criticism, political and social commentary, and theological reflection (*Life of Jesus*, 1936). He wrote vigorously in opposition to fascism of all kinds. He opposed General Franco in Spain, the Italian invasion of Ethiopia, and, in his own country, stood with the Resistance to Nazism. After the war, he was a strong supporter of French decolonization in Africa and Southeast

Asia. His newspaper column, "Bloc-Notes," was his primary venue for commentary from the 1950s on and won him a wide audience.

François Mauriac's status in French letters was recognized in 1952, when he was awarded the Nobel Prize for Literature. The Nobel Committee noted that he was being recognized "for the penetrating psychology and artistic intensity with which he has expressed the drama of human life in his novels."

François Mauriac died in 1970 in Paris.

Readers,

We'd like to hear from you! What other classic Catholic novels would you like to see in the Loyola Classics series? Please e-mail your suggestions and comments to **loyolaclassics@loyolapress.com** or mail them to:

Loyola Classics
Loyola Press
3441 N. Ashland Avenue
Chicago, IL 60657